MEL BAY PRESENTS
SONGS OF SCOTLAND

86 Favourite Scottish Songs and Ballads

By Jerry Silverman

A Note From Jerry Silverman

The songs in this collection, in some small way, tell the history of the Scottish people. They pass from Highland broadswords to nuclear submarines by way of outlaws, heroes, lords and ladies, common folk, workers, sailors, and lovers.

A notable contribution to Scottish balladry was made by the Jacobite Rebellions of 1715 and 1745. These rebellions were conducted by the adherents of James II ("Jacobus" in Latin — hence the term "Jacobite") and his descendents, who took as their first aim the restoration of the Stuarts to the throne of England and Scotland. The most unforgettable figure to come from these doomed efforts was the son of James — Prince Charles Edward. The exploits of Bonnie Prince Charlie, real and exaggerated, are celebrated in a notable body of beautiful songs.

Then came Robert Burns (1759–1796), whose lyrical commentaries on virtually every aspect of Scottish life represent an unparalleled record of the social, philosophical, and cultural thinking of the people of his time.

Finally, the Scottish republican songs of the mid-20th century follow the rich mainstream of Scottish satirical irreverence for authority, as expressed earlier by Burns and the generations of anonymous bards that preceded and followed him.

The Cassette

Excerpts from all the songs, sung by Jerry Silverman, will help those who would like to sing them but whose note-reading ability may not be quite up to the task.

Contents

Traditional Ballads

Annie Laurie 16
The Barnyards of Delgaty 28
The Blantyre Explosion 26
The Blue Bells of Scotland 21
The Bonnie Earl of Murray 22
Bonnie George Campbell 33
The Bonnie House o' Airlie 48
The Bonnie Ship, the Diamond 27
Brown Adam, the Smith 50
The Calton Weaver 10
Comin' Through the Rye 17
The Dowie Dens of Yarrow 13
Dumbarton's Drums 3
The Four Marys 11
The Great Silkie 9
The Gypsy Rover 45
Haud Yer Tongue Dear Sally 34
Henry Martin 24
Hurree Hurroo 7
Jamie Raeburn's Farewell 32
Johnie Blunt 29
Lang A-Growing 12
Loch Lomond 15
Lord Randal 46
Lowe Bonnie 8
The Lowlands of Holland 52
MacPherson's Farewell 4
Maiden of the Dark Brown Hair 31
Maids, When You're Young Never Wed an Old
  Man 36
O, Are Ye Sleepin,' Maggie? 35
The Pride of Glencoe 40
Rigs o' Rye 39
Rothesay-O 20
Sir Patrick Spens 41
Son David 44
To the Begging I Will Go 42
The Trooper and the Maid 6
Waillie, Waillie 5
The Wee Cooper O'Fife 23
The Wee Wee Man 43
Weel May the Keel Row 25
Where the Gaudy Runs 14
The Work of the Weavers 30

The Jacobite Rebellions

Bonnie Charlie's Now Awa' 66
Bonnie Dundee 53
Came Ye O'er Frae France? 58
Donald MacGillavry 60
The Haughs of Cromdale 56
Johnnie Cope 64
My Bonnie Moorhen 69
The Piper o' Dundee 62
Skye Boat Song 65
There's Three Brave Loyal Fellows 54
This Is No My Ain House 70
Wae's Me for Prince Charlie 68
The Wee, Wee German Lairdie 59
Will Ye Go to Sherrifmuir? 63

Songs of Bobbie Burns

Auld Lang Syne 81
The Bonniest Lass 80
Braw Lads o' Galla Water 104
Charlie Is My Darling 74
Corn Rigs 94
Flow Gently, Sweet Afton 86
For the Sake o' Somebody 90
Green Grow the Rashes, O 82
Guidwife, Count the Lawin' 76
Hey, the Dusty Miller 76
The Highland Widow's Lament 101
I'm O'er Young 89
Is There for Honest Poverty
  (A Man's a Man for a' That) 79
John Anderson, My Jo 102
John Highlandman 84
Kellyburn Braes 103
My Dowrie's the Jewel 92
My Luve Is Like a Red, Red Rose 77
O, Whistle an' I'll Come to Ye, My Lad 85
Once More I Hail Thee 75
Scots Wha Hae 105
Sodger Laddie 98
Such a Parcel of Rogues 73
Wanderin' Willie 99
We're a' Noddin' 93
Ye Jacobites by Name 72

Republican Broadsides

The Coronation Coronach 110
Ding Dong Dollar 111
The Wee Magic Stane 108

Dumbarton's Drums

The first appearance of the text in print was 1724, in the first volume of Allan Ramsay's *Tea-Table Miscellany*. In 1733 it appeared with text and tune in William Thompson's *Orpheus Caledonius*.

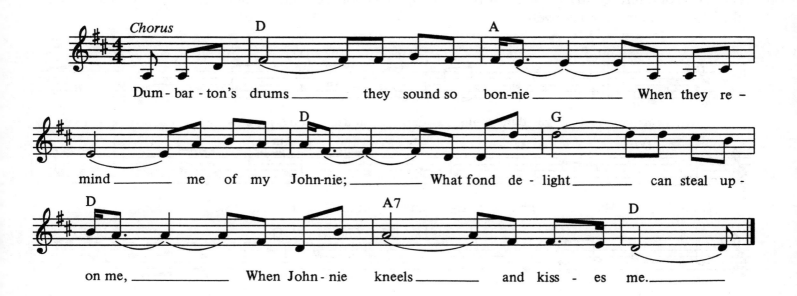

Dum-bar-ton's drums _____ they sound so bon-nie _____ When they re-mind _____ me of my John-nie; _____ What fond de-light _____ can steal up-on me, _____ When John-nie kneels _____ and kiss-es me. _____

     D   A
Across the fields of bounding heather,
             D
Dumbarton tolls the hour of pleasure;
   G   D
A song of love that has no measure,
         A7   D
When Johnnie kneels and sings to me. *Chorus*

         D   A
'Tis he alone that can delight me,
               D
His graceful eye, it doth invite me;
          G   D
And when his tender arms enfold me,
         A7   D
The blackest night doth turn and see. *Chorus*

         D   A
My love he is a handsome laddie,
               D
And though he is Dumbarton's caddie,
       G   D
Some day I'll be a captain's lady,
       A7   D
When Johnnie tends his vow to me. *Chorus*

caddie—servant

MacPherson's Farewell

James MacPherson, a daring highwayman, was apprehended for robbery at Keith Market and haled before the Sheriff of Banff on November 1, 1700. He was condemned to be hanged at the assizes of Inverness and was executed at the Cross of Banff on November 10. While awaiting execution, he is said to have composed this tune, which he called his own Lament or Farewell.

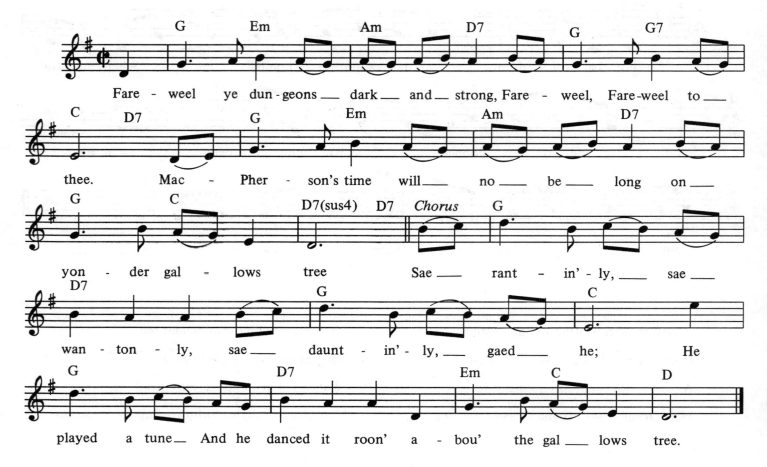

Fare-weel ye dun-geons dark and strong, Fare-weel, Fare-weel to thee. Mac-Pher-son's time will no be long on yon-der gal-lows tree Sae rant-in'-ly, sae wan-ton-ly, sae daunt-in'-ly, gaed he; He played a tune And he danced it roon' a-bou' the gal lows tree.

	G	Em	Am	D7
It was by a woman's treacherous hand				
	G	G7	C	D7
That I was condemned to dee.				
	G	Em	Am	D7
Below a ledge at a window she stood,				
	G	C	D7sus4	D7
And a blanket she threw o'er me.				*Chorus*

	G	Em	Am	D7
Untie these bands from off my hands,				
	G	G7	C	D7
And gie to me my sword,				
	G	Em	Am	D7
An' there's no' a man in all Scotland,				
	G	C	D7sus4	D7
But I'll brave him at a word.				*Chorus*

	G	Em	Am	D7
The Laird o' Grant, that Highland sant,				
	G	G7	C	D7
That first laid hands on me.				
	G	Em	Am	D7
He played the cause on Peter Broon				
	G	C	D7sus4	D7
To let MacPherson dee.				*Chorus*

	G	Em	Am	D7
The reprieve was comin' o'er the brig o' Banff,				
	G	G7	C	D7
To let MacPherson free;				
	G	Em	Am	D7
But they pit the clock a quarter afore,				
	G	C	D7sus4	D7
And hanged him to the tree.				*Chorus*

brig—bridge

4

G Em Am D7	G Em Am D7
There's some come here to see me hanged,	He took the fiddle into both o' his hands,
G G7 C D7	G G7 C D7
And some to buy my fiddle,	And he broke it o'er a stone.
G Em Am D7	G Em Am D7
But before that I do part wi' her	Says, "There's nae ither hand shall play on thee,
G C D7sus4 D7	G C D7sus4 D7
I'll brak her thro' the middle. *Chorus*	When I am dead and gone." *Chorus*

G Em Am D7
O little did my mother think
G G7 C
When first she cradled me,
G Em Am D7
That I would turn a rovin' boy
G C D7sus4 D7
And die on the gallows tree.   *Chorus*

Waillie, Waillie

When cock - le shells_____ Turn sil - ver bells_____
When ros - es grow_____ 'Neath win - ter snow,_____
(3rd time) But when love's old, _____ It grow - eth cold,_____

____ Then will my love re - turn to_____ me.
____ Then will my love re - turn to_____ me.   *To next strain*
____ And fades a - way like morn - ing_____ dew.   *Fine*

Wail - lie, Oh wail - lie, But love it is bon - nie____

____ A lit - tle while when it_____ is new.

The Trooper and the Maid

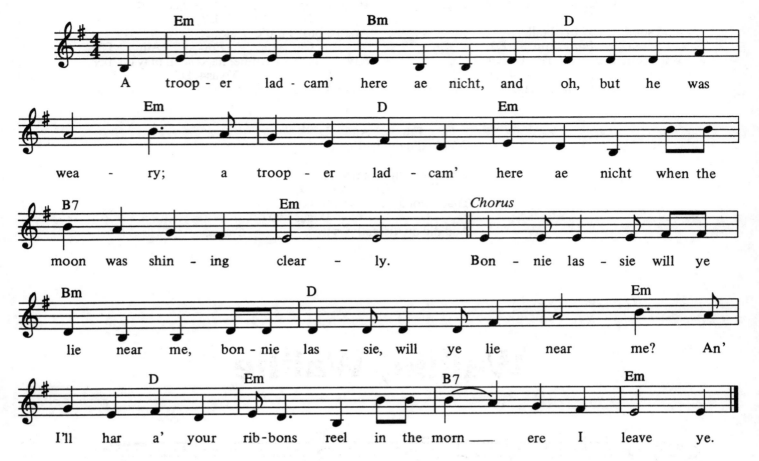

A troop-er lad-cam' here ae nicht, and oh, but he was wea-ry; a troop-er lad-cam' here ae nicht when the moon was shin-ing clear-ly.

Chorus

Bon-nie las-sie will ye lie near me, bon-nie las-sie, will ye lie near me? An' I'll har a' your rib-bons reel in the morn ——— ere I leave ye.

Em   Bm
She's ta'en the horse by the halter right,
D   Em
And led it to the stable;
D   Em
She's gi'en him oats and hay to eat,
B7   Em
As muckle as he was able. *Chorus*

Em   Bm
She's ta'en the sodger by the lily-white hand,
D   Em
And led him to her chamber;
D   Em
She's gi'en him a stoup o'wine to drink,
B7   Em
His love it fleered like aimber. *Chorus*

Em   Bm
She's made her bed baith lang and wide,
D   Em
She's made it like a lady;
D   Em
She's ta'en her wee coatie ower her heid,
B7   Em
Said, "Sodger, are ye ready?" *Chorus*

Em   Bm
And he's ta'en aff his belted coat,
D   Em
Likewise his hat and feather,
D   Em
And leaned his sword against the door,
B7   Em
And noo he's doon aside her. *Chorus*

Em   Bm
They hadna been but an hour in bed,
D   Em
An hour but and a quarter,
D   Em
When the drum cam' soundin' up the street,
B7   Em
And ilka beat was shorter. *Chorus*

Em   Bm
"It's up, up, up, and our colonel cries,
D   Em
It's up, up, up, and away then;
D   Em
I maun sheathe my sword in its scabbard case,
B7   Em
For tomorrow's our battle day then." *Chorus*

ae—one	**fleered**—flared	**ilka**—every	**ower**—over
aimber—amber	**glen**—given	**muckle**—much	**stoup**—jug

Em   Bm
"And when will ye come back again,
D   Em
My ain dear sodger laddie?
D   Em
When will ye come back again,
B7   Em
And be your bairn's daddie?" *Chorus*

Em   Bm
"O, haud your tongue, my bonnie wee lass,
D   Em
Dinna let this pairtin' grieve ye;
Em D Em
When heather cowes grow ousen bows,
B7   Em
Bonnie lassie, I'll come and see ye." *Chorus*

Em   Bm
She's ta'en her wee coatie ower her heid,
D   Em
And followed him up to Stirlin',
D   Em
She's grown sae fu' that she couldna boo,
B7   Em
And he's left her in Dunfermline. *Chorus*

Em   Bm
It's breid and cheese for carles and dames,
D   Em
And oats and hay for horses;
D Em
A cup of tea for auld maids,
B7   Em
And bonnie lads for lasses. *Chorus*

carles—men **cowes**—bushes, twigs **dinna**—don't **ousen bows**—oxen yokes

Hurree Hurroo

Hebrides Islands

Chorus
Hur-ree hur-roo, my bon-ny wee lass, Hur-ree___ hur-roo,___ my fair one; And will you come a-way,___ my love,___ To be my own, my fair___ one.___ *Fine*

Verses
Smil-ing the land, smil-ing the sea, Sweet was the smell of the heath-er, Would we were yon-der, just you and me,___ The two of us to-geth-er.___

All the day long, out by the peat, Then by the shore in the gloam-ing, Trip-ping it light-ly with danc-ing feet,___ Then we to-geth-er roam-ing.___

Lowe Bonnie

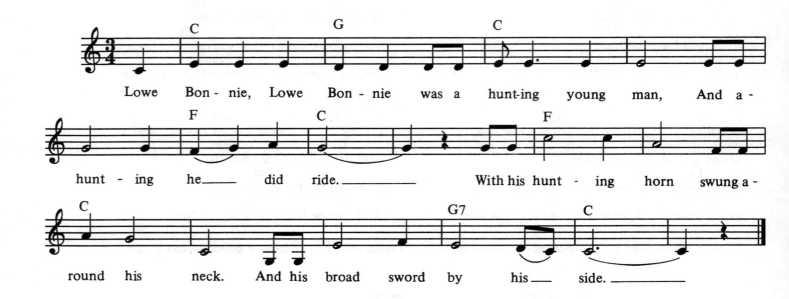

Lowe Bon - nie, Lowe Bon - nie was a hunt-ing young man, And a - hunt - ing he____ did ride.____ With his hunt - ing horn swung a - round his neck. And his broad sword by his __ side.____

He hunted 'til he came to his old true love,
In a lightnin' he tangled at his reigns.
No one was so ready but his old true love
To ride and say call in.

"Call in call in, Lowe Bonnie," she cried,
"And stay all night with me.
A burning porridge you shall receive,
And a drink of white chocolate tea."

He says, "I will call in and I will sit down,
But I haven't got a moment to stay.
There's one little girl in this whole round town
That I love better than thee."

Oh, it's while she was sitting all on his lap,
He was kissing her so sweet,
A little pen knife was so keen and sharp,
She wounded him so deep.

"Don't die don't die, Lowe Bonnie," she cried,
"Don't die, don't die so soon.
I sent for the doctors in the whole round town,
For one who can heal your wounds."

"How can I live, how can I live?
You've wounded me so deep.
I think I feel my own heart's blood
A-dropping on my feet."

The Great Silkie

Silkies are legendary seal-men who appear on land in human form, often in search of brides. This generally leads to all sorts of complications.... Sule Skerry is a sea rock 35 miles west of Orkney.

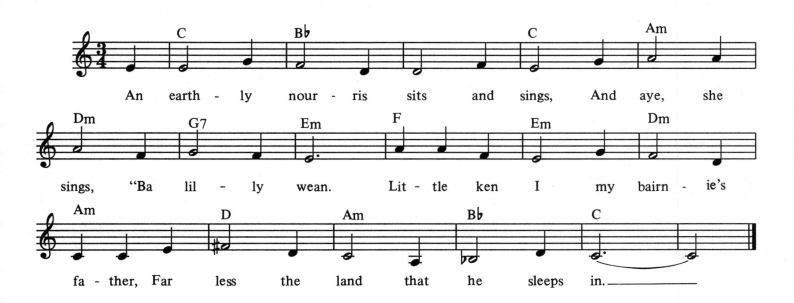

An earth - ly nour - ris sits and sings, And aye, she sings, "Ba lil - ly wean. Lit - tle ken I my bairn - ie's fa - ther, Far less the land that he sleeps in. _____

       C B♭   C
Then in he steps to her bedside,
      Am Dm G7   Em
And a grumbly guest I'm sure was he.
     F   Em   Dm   Am
Saying, "Here I am, thy bairnie's father,
  D   Am B♭ C
Although I be not comely.

       C B♭   C
"I am a man upon the land,
      Am Dm G7   Em
And I am a silkie in the sea.
     F   Em   Dm   Am
And when I'm far and far from land,
    D Am B♭   C
My home it is in Sule Skerry."

       C B♭   C
Then he has taken a purse of gold,
     Am Dm G7   Em
And he has put it upon her knee.
       F   Em   Dm   Am
Saying, "Give to me my little young son,
    D Am B♭   C
And take thee up thy nourris fee.

         C B♭   C
It shall come to pass on a summer's day,
       Am Dm G7   Em
When the sun shines hot on every stone,
      F   Em   Dm   Am
That I shall take my little young son,
     D   Am B♭   C
And teach him how to swim the foam.

        C   B♭   C
"And thou shall marry a proud gunner,
      Am Dm   G7   Em
And a proud gunner, I'm sure he'll be.
      F   Em   Dm   Am
And the very first shot that e'er he'll shoot,
     D   Am B♭   C
Will kill both my young son and me."

      C B♭   C
"Alas, alas," the maiden cried,
      Am Dm   G7   Em
"This weary fate's been laid for me."
      F   Em   Dm   Am
And then she said, and then she said,
     D Am B♭   C
"I'll bury me in Sule Skerry."

bairnie—baby   **nourris**—nursemaid

The Calton Weaver

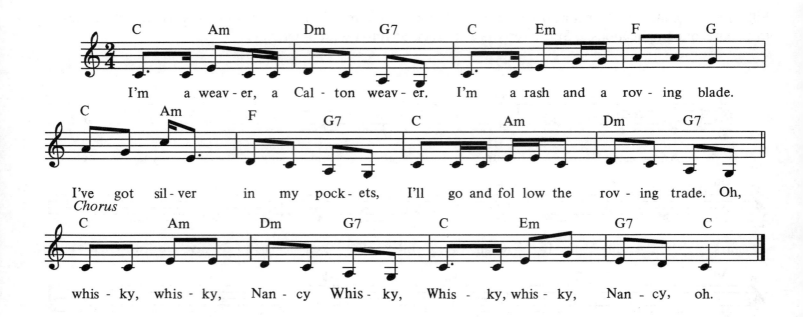

I'm a weav-er, a Cal-ton weav-er. I'm a rash and a rov-ing blade.

I've got sil-ver in my pock-ets, I'll go and fol low the rov-ing trade. Oh,
Chorus

whis-ky, whis-ky, Nan-cy Whis-ky, Whis-ky, whis-ky, Nan-cy, oh.

      C   Am Dm G7
As I cam' in by Glesca city,
      C   Em   F   G
Nancy Whisky I chanced to smell,
C   Am   F   G7
I gaed in, sat doon beside her,
C   Am Dm G7
Seven lang years lo'ed her well.   *Chorus*

        C Am   Dm   G7
"C'wa, landlady, whit's the lawin'?
      C   Em   F   G
Tell me whit there is to pay."
      C   Am   F   G7
"Fifteen shillings is the reckoning,
      C   Am   Dm   G7
Pay me quickly and go away." *Chorus*

        C   Am   Dm   G7
The mair I kissed her the mair I lo'ed her,
        C   Em   F   G
The mair I kissed her the mair she smiled,
      C   Am   F   G7
And I forgot my mither's teaching,
      C   Am   Dm   G7
Nancy soon had me beguiled. *Chorus*

        C   Am   Dm   G7
As I went oot by Glesca city,
      C   Em   F   G
Nancy Whisky, I chanced to smell;
C   Am   F   G7
I gaed in, drank four and sixpence,
C   Am   Dm   G7
A't was left was a crooked scale. *Chorus*

      C   Am Dm   G7
I woke early in the morning,
        C   Em   F   G
To slake my drouth it was my need;
C   Am   F   G7
I tried to rise but I wasna able,
      C   Am   Dm   G7
Nancy had me by the heid. *Chorus*

        C   Am   Dm   G7
I'll gang back to the Calton weaving,
        C   Em   F   G
I'll surely mak' the shuttles fly;
C   Am   F   G7
I'll mak' mair at the Calton weaving
        C   Am   Dm   G7
Than ever I did in a roving way. *Chorus*

             C   Am   Dm   G7
Come all ye weavers, Calton weavers,
        C   Em   F   G
A' ye weavers where e'er ye be;
         C   Am   F   G7
Beware of Whisky, Nancy Whisky,
         C   Am   Dm   G7
She'll ruin you as she ruined me. *Chorus*

The Four Marys

Mary Hamilton, the tragic heroine of this old ballad was supposedly one of "four Marys" who were ladies-in-waiting to the "fifth Mary", Mary, Queen of Scots.   However, the name of Mary Hamilton does not appear in any official records of the time.   Other versions of this ballad (placed around 1563) have Mary bearing an illegitimate child as a result of an affair with Lord Darnley, the Queen's husband.   She drowns the baby and is subsequently hanged for her crime.

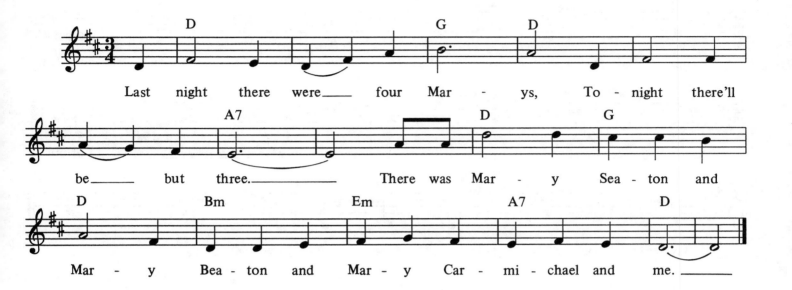

Last night there were____ four Mar - ys, To - night there'll be____ but three.____ There was Mar - y Sea - ton and Mar - y Bea - ton and Mar - y Car - mi - chael and me. ____

D   G   D
Oh, often have I dressed my queen
               A7
And put on her braw silk gown,
D   G   D Bm
But all the thanks I've got tonight ,
  Em   A7   D
Is to be hanged in Edinborough Town.

D   G   D
Oh, little did my mother know,
               A7
The day she cradled me,
D   G   D Bm
The land I was to travel in,
  Em   A7   D
The death I was to dee.

D   G   D
Full often have I dressed my queen,
              A7
Put gold upon her hair,
D   G   D Bm
But I have got for my reward
Em   A7   D
The gallows to be my share.

D   G   D
Oh, happy, happy, is the maid
              A7
That's born of beauty free;
D   G   D   Bm
Oh, it was my rosy dimpled cheeks
  Em   A7   D
That's been the devil to me.

D   G   D
They'll tie a kerchief around my eyes,
          A7
That I may not see to dee,
D   G   D   Bm
And they'll never tell my father or mother
  Em   A7   D
But that I'm across the sea.

Repeat verse one.

11

Lang A-Growing

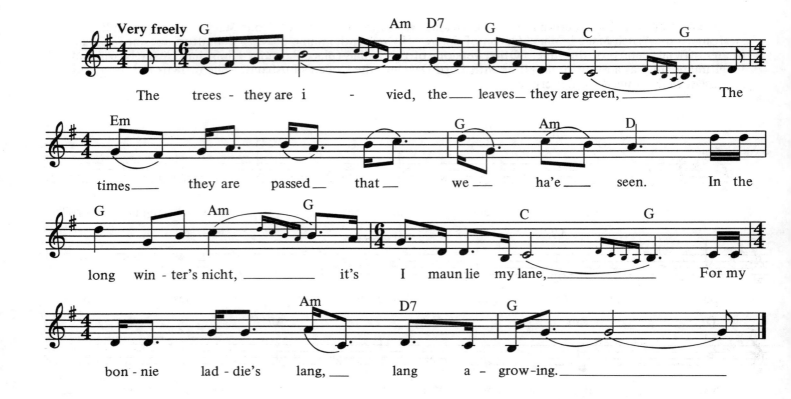

The trees - they are i - vied, the leaves they are green, The
times they are passed that we ha'e seen. In the
long win - ter's nicht, it's I maun lie my lane, For my
bon - nie lad - die's lang, lang a - grow-ing.

G   Am D7   G   C   G
O, father, dear father, ye ha'e done me muckle wrang,
Em   G   Am   D
For ye ha'e wedded me to a lad that's ower young,
G   Am G   C G
For he is but twelve and I am thirteen,
     Am   D7   G
And my bonnie laddie's lang, lang a-growing.

G   Am D7   G   C   G
O, dochter, dear dochter, I ha'e done ye nae wrang,
Em   G   Am   D
For I ha'e wedded you to a noble lord's son,
G   Am G   C G
And he shall be the laird and you shall wait on,
     Am   D7   G
And a' the time your lad'll be a-growing.

G   Am D7   G   C G
O, father, dear father, if you think it will fit,
Em   G   Am   D
We'll send him to the school for a year or twa yet,
G   Am G   C G
And we'll tie a green ribbon around about his bonnet,
     Am   D7   G
And that'll be a token that's he married.

G   Am D7 G   C G
O, father, dear father, and if it please you,
Em   G Am D
I'll cut my long hair abune my broo;
G   Am G   C G
Vest, coat and breeks I will gladly put on,
     Am   D7   G
And I to the school will gang wi' him.

G   Am D7   G   C G
She's made him a sark o' the holland so fine,
Em   G Am D
And she has sewed it wi' her fingers ain;
G   Am G   C G
And aye she loot the tears doon fa'
     Am   D7   G
Crying, my bonnie laddie's lang, lang a-growing.

G   Am D7 G   C G
In his twelfth year, he was a married man,
Em   G Am D
And in his thirteenth he had gotten her a son;
G   Am G   C G
And in his fourteenth, his grave it grew green,
     Am   D7   G
And that's put an end to his growing.

abuhe my broo—above my brow   **muckle**—much   **sark**—shirt   **wrang**—wrong

The Dowie Dens of Yarrow

First published in *Minstrelsy of the Scottish Border,* by Sir Walter Scott, in 1830.

There was a la-dy in the north, I ne'er could find her mar-row; She was court-ed by nine gen-tle-men, And a plough-boy lad frae Yar-row.

Am G Am
These nine sat drinking at the wine,
 F   Am Em
Sat drinking wine at Yarrow;
   C   G
They ha'e made a vow amang themselves
 Am Em Am
To fecht for her on Yarrow.

Am   G   Am
As he walked up yon high, high hills,
 F   Am Em
And doon by the houms o' Yarrow;
 C   G
There he saw nine armed men
  Am Em Am
Come to fecht wi' him on Yarrow.

 Am   G Am
There's nine o' you, there's one o' me,
 F   Am Em
It's an unequal marrow;
  C   G
But I'll fecht you a' one by one
 Am Em Am
On the dowie dens o' Yarrow.

 Am   G Am
And there they flew and there he slew,
 F   Am Em
And there he wounded sairly;
  C   G
Till her brither, John, came in beyond
  Am Em Am
And pierced his hairt most foully.

      Am   G Am
"O, father dear, ye've seiven sons,
      F   Am Em
Ye may wed them a' tomorrow,
       C   G
But the fairest flooer amang them a'
      Am Em Am
Was the lad I wooed on Yarrow;

Am   G   Am
"O father, dear, I dreamed a dream,
 F   Am Em
A dream i' dule and sorrow;
  C   G
I dreamed I was pu'ing the heather bells
   Am Em Am
On the dowie dens o' Yarrow."

Am   G   Am
"O, dochter dear, I read your dream,
 F   Am Em
I doubt it will bring sorrow;
  C   G
For your lover John, lies pale and wan
   Am Em Am
On the dowie dens o' Yarrow;

Am   G   Am
As she walked up yon high, high hill,
 F   Am Em
And doon by the houms o' Yarrow;
 C   G
There she saw her lover dear
   Am Em Am
Lying pale and wan on Yarrow.

Am   G   Am
Her hair it being three-quarters long,
    F   Am Em
The colour it was yellow,
   C   G
She wrappit it roond his middle sae sma'
  Am Em Am
And bore him doon to Yarrow.

fecht—fight **marrow**—spouse, helpmate

13

Where the Gaudy Runs

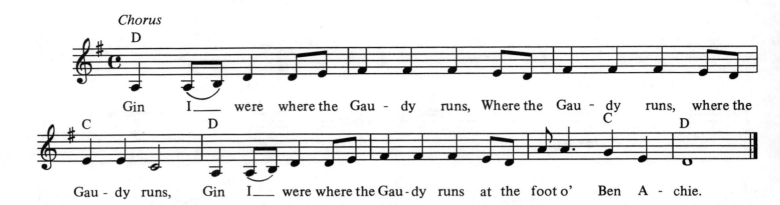

Chorus

Gin I were where the Gau-dy runs, Where the Gau-dy runs, where the Gau-dy runs, Gin I were where the Gau-dy runs at the foot o' Ben A-chie.

D
I never hd but two richt loves,
C
But two richt loves, but two richt loves.
D
I never had but two richt loves,
C **D**
And they both dearly loved me. *Chorus*

D
The tane was killed at the Lowren Fair,
C
At the Lowren Fair, at the Lowren Fair.
D
The tane was killed at the Lowren Fair,
C **D**
And the other drowned in the Dee. *Chorus*

D
They crowded in so thick on him,
C
So thick on him, so thick on him.
D
They crowded in so thick on him,
C **D**
That he could nae fight or flee. *Chorus*

D
Had they gi'en my laddie mon for mon,
C
Mon for mon, o, mon for mon,
D
Had they gi'en my laddie mon for mon,
C **D**
Or yet a mon for three. *Chorus*

D
He would nae ha'e lain so low,
C
Lain sae low, lain sae low.
D
He would nae ha'e lain so low,
C **D**
At the foot o' yonder tree. *Chorus*

D
He bought for me a bra new goon,
C
A bra new goon, a bra new goon.
D
He bought for me a bra new goon,
C **D**
And ribbons to bask it wi.' *Chorus*

D
I bought for him a linen fine,
C
A linen fine, a linen fine.
D
I bought for him a linen fine,
C **D**
His windin' sheet to be. *Chorus*

D
O, that's twice I hae been a bride,
C
Been a bride, been a bride.
D
O, that's twice I hae been a bride,
C **D**
But a wife I ne'er shall be. *Chorus*

Ben—Mount   **bra**—pretty   **goon**—gown   **tane**—one

Loch Lomond

Words by Lady John Scott

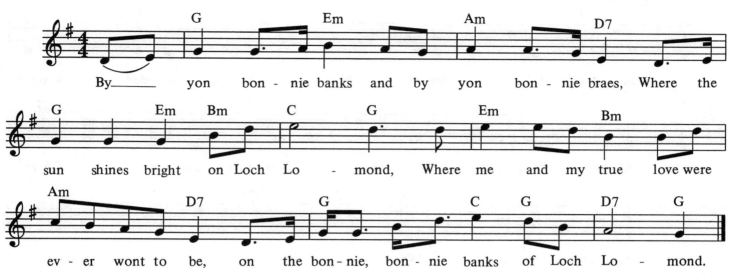

By____ yon bon - nie banks and by yon bon - nie braes, Where the sun shines bright on Loch Lo - mond, Where me and my true love were ev - er wont to be, on the bon - nie, bon - nie banks of Loch Lo - mond.

Chorus:

     G   Em   Am   D7
O, you'll take the high road and I'll take the low road,
     G   Em Bm C G
And I'll be in Scotland before you.
     Em   Bm   Am   D7
But me and my true love will never meet again
     G   C G   D7 G
On the bonnie, bonnie banks of Loch Lomond.

     G   Em Am   D7
I mind where we parted in yon shady glen,
     G   Em Bm   C G
On the steep, steep side of Ben Lomond,
     Em   Bm   Am   D7
Where the deep purple hue the Highlands we view,
     G   C G D7 G
And the moon coming out in the gloaming. *Chorus*

     G   Em Am   D7
The wee birdies sing and the wild flowers spring,
     G   Em Bm   C G
And in sunshine the waters are sleeping.
     Em   Bm   Am   D7
But the broken heart will ken no second spring again,
     G   C G D7 G
And the world does not know how we are greeting. *Chorus*

Ben—Mount(ain)   **braes**—hillocks

Annie Laurie

By William Douglas

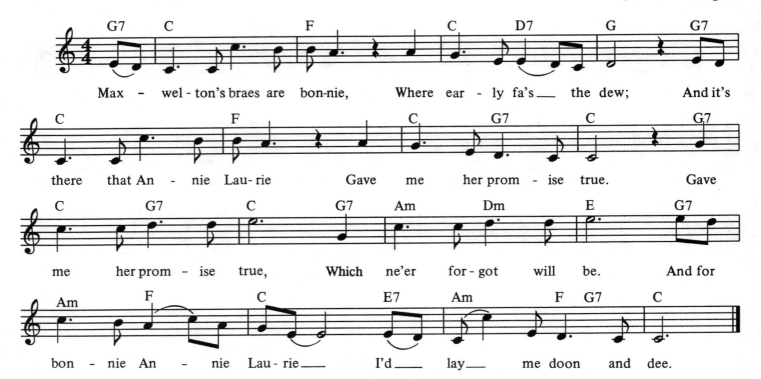

Max - wel-ton's braes are bon-nie, Where ear - ly fa's __ the dew; And it's

there that An - nie Lau-rie Gave me her prom - ise true. Gave

me her prom - ise true, Which ne'er for-got will be. And for

bon - nie An - nie Lau - rie __ I'd __ lay __ me doon and dee.

G7 C   F
Her brow is like the snawdrift,
      C   D7   G
Her throat is like the swan,
G7 C   F
Her face it is the fairest
       C   G7   C
That e'er the sun shone on.
G7 C   G7   C
That e'er the sun shone on,
G7   Am   Dm   E
And dark blue is her e'e.
G7   Am   F   C
And for bonnie Annie Laurie
E7 Am   F G7   C
I'd lay me doon and dee.

G7 C   F
Like dew on the gowan lying,
      C   D7 G
Is the fa' o' her fairy feet,
G7   C   F
And like winds in summer sighing,
       C   G7   C
Her voice is low and sweet.
G7 C   G7   C
Her voice is low and sweet,
G7   Am   Dm   E
And she's a' the world to me.
G7   Am   F   C
And for bonnie Annie Laurie
E7 Am   F G7   C
I'd lay me doon and dee.

Comin' Through the Rye

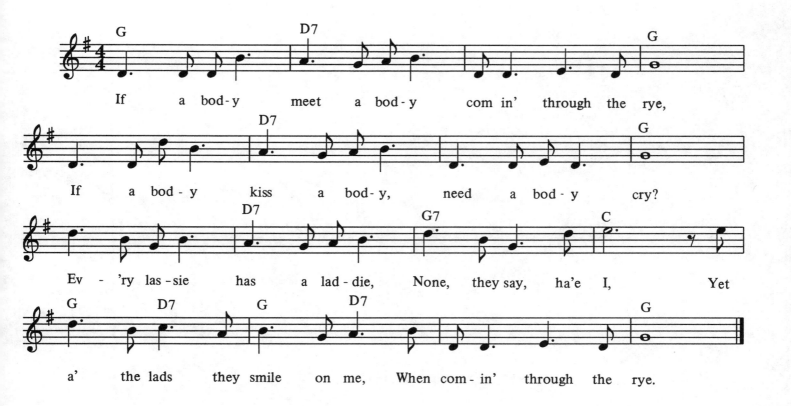

If a bod-y meet a bod-y com in' through the rye,

If a bod-y kiss a bod-y, need a bod-y cry?

Ev - 'ry las -sie has a lad - die, None, they say, ha'e I, Yet

a' the lads they smile on me, When com - in' through the rye.

G   D7
Gin a body meet a body,
           G
Comin' frae the toon,
        D7
Gin a body greet a body,
        G
Need a body froon?
             D7
Among the train there is a swain,
    G7   C
I dearly love mysel',
        G   D7   G   D7
But what's his name or what's his hame,
         G
I donna care to tell.

Rothesay-O

This saga of a rough weekend in Scotland's most popular holiday resort is based on a country song, "The Tinker's Wedding," written by William Watt, a weaver from West Linton, Peebleshire, in 1792. The parody followed soon after as a music-hall piece and has been popular ever since.

A sodger lad named Rutherglen Will,
    C   *Dm*   *C*
Wha's regiment's lyin' at Barn Hill,
    Bb
Went off wi' a tanner to get a jill
    C   *Dm* *C*
In a public hoose in Rothesay, O.
    G7   *C*
Said he, "By Christ, I'd like to sing."
    C7   *F*   *C*
Said I, "Ye'll no' dae sic a thing."
    G7   *C*
He said, "Clear the room and I'll mak' a ring
    F   *C7*   *F*   *C*
And I'll fecht them all in Rothesay, O." *Chorus*
    Dm   *G7*   *C*

    C   *Dm*   *C*
I' search of lodgins we did slide,
To find a place where we could bide;
    Bb
There was eichty-twa o' us inside
    C   *Dm* *C*
In a single room in Rothesay, O.
    G7   *C*
We a' lay doon to tak' our ease,
    C7   *F*   *C*
When somebody happened for to sneeze,
    G7   *C*
And he wakened half a million fleas
    F   *C7*   *F*   *C*
In that single room in Rothesay. O. *Chorus*
    Dm   *G7*   *C*

20

           C   Dm   C
There were several different kinds of bugs,
                  B♭
Some had feet like dyers' clogs,
           C   Dm   C
And they sat on the bed and they cockit their lugs
            G7   C
And cried, " Hurrah for Rothesay, O!"
            G7   F   C
I said, "I think we should elope!"
            G7   C
So we went and joined the Band O' Hope,
            F   C7   F   C
But the polis wouldna let us stop
    Dm   G7   C
Another nicht in Rothesay, O.   *Chorus*

The Blue Bells of Scotland

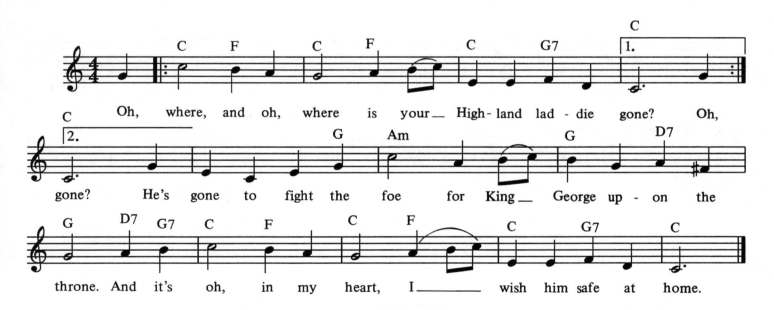

Oh, where, and oh, where is your High-land lad-die gone? Oh, gone? He's gone to fight the foe for King George up-on the throne. And it's oh, in my heart, I wish him safe at home.

        C   F   C   F   C   G7   C
Oh where, and oh where did your Highland laddie dwell?   (2)
             G Am   G   D7   G
He dwelt in merry Scotland at the sign of the Blue Bell.
D7 G7 C F   C   FC   G7   C
And it's oh, in my heart, I love my laddie well.

        C F   C F   C   G7   C
Suppose, and suppose your Highland lad should die?   (2)
             G Am   G   D7   G
The bagpipes shall play o'er him and I'll lay me down and cry,
D7 G7 C F   C   FC   G7   C
But it's oh, in my heart, I wish he may not die.

21

The Bonnie Earl of Murray

The earldom of Murray (or Moray) was one of the seven original earldoms of Scotland. Its lands correspond roughly to the modern counties of Inverness and Ross. It dates back to about 1314, when Sir Thomas Randolph, a nephew of King Robert Bruce, was created earl of Moray. By the 15th century, the earldom had shifted to an illegitimate branch of the royal house of Stuart. The earldom of Huntly was conferred upon the Gordon family in 1449. George Huntly, the fifth earl of Huntly, found himself engaged in a private war with the Grants and the Mackintoshes, who were assisted by the earls of Atholl and Murray. On February 8, 1592, Huntly set fire to the castle of James Stuart, "the bonnie earl of Murray," at Donibristle in Fife, and stabbed him to death with his own hand.

Ye high-lands and ye low-lands, ___ O where ha' ye been? They have slain the Earl of Mur-ray, ___ And laid him on the green. He was a braw gal-lant, ___ And he rode ___ at the ring And the bon-nie Earl of Mur-ray, ___ He might have been a king.

Bm
"Now wae be to thee, Huntly.
   Em
And wherefore did you sae?
 C
I bade you bring him wi' ye,
   Em
But forbade you him to slay."
    G
  He was a braw gallant,
     D
  And he play'd at the ba,'
     C   G
And the bonnie Earl of Murray,
    Am7   D
Was the flower of them a.'

Bm
He was a braw gallant,
    Em
And he play'd at the glove,
    C
And the bonnie Earl of Murray,
    Em
He was the Queen's own love.
     G
  Oh, lang will his lady
      D
  Look o'er the castle down,
     C   G
E'er she see the Earl of Murray,
    Am7   D
Come sounding through the town.

The Wee Cooper O'Fife

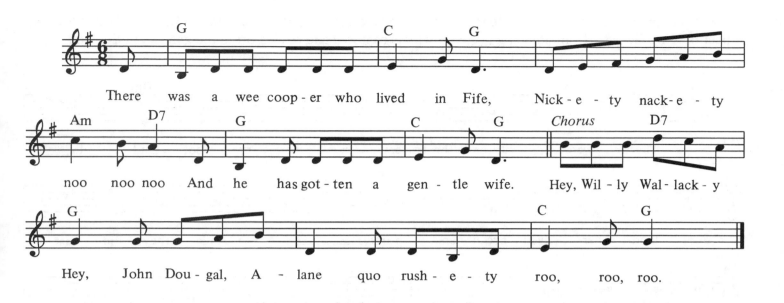

There was a wee coop-er who lived in Fife, Nick-e-ty nack-e-ty noo noo noo And he has got-ten a gen-tle wife. Hey, Wil-ly Wal-lack-y

Hey, John Dou-gal, A - lane quo rush-e-ty roo, roo, roo.

G   C G
She wouldna bake, she wouldna brew,
     Am   D7
Nickety nackety noo noo noo,
G   C G
For the spoilin' o' her comely hue. *Chorus*

G   C G
She wouldna card, she wouldna spin,
     Am   D7
Nickety nackety noo noo noo,
G   C G
For the shamin' o' her gentle kin. *Chorus*

G   C G
She wouldna wash, she wouldna wring,
     Am   D7
Nickety nackety noo noo noo,
G   C G
For the spoilin' o' her golden ring. *Chorus*

G   C G
The cooper has gone to his wool pack,
     Am   D7
Nickety nackety noo noo noo,
G   C G
He laid a sheep skin across his wife's back. *Chorus*

G   C G
I wouldna thrash ye for your gentle kin.
     Am   D7
Nickety nackety noo noo noo,
G   C G
But I will thrash my own sheep skin. *Chorus*

G   C G
A' ye wha hae gotten a gentle wife,
     Am   D7
Nickety nackety noo noo noo,
G   C G
Send ye for the Wee Cooper O' Fife. *Chorus*

23

Henry Martin

In some versions of this pirate ballad, Henry Martin (or Andrew Bartin) defeats and taunts Captain Charles Stewart, officer of King George III. In others, it is Henry who is captured and hauled off to the gallows in England.

The lot it fell upon Henry Martin,
The youngest of all the three,
That he should turn robber all on the salt sea, salt sea, salt sea,
For to maintain his two brothers and he.

He had not been sailing but a long winter's night,
And part of a short winter's day,
When he espied a lofty stout ship, stout ship, stout ship,
Come a-bibbing down on him straightway.

"Hello, hello," cried Henry Martin,
"What makes you sail so nigh?"
"I'm a rich merchant ship bound for fair London Town,
London Town, London Town,
Will you please for to let me pass by?"

"Oh, no, oh no," cried Henry Martin,
"That thing it never can be,
For I have turned robber all on the salt sea, salt sea, salt sea,
For to maintain my two brothers and me."

With broadside and broadside and at it they went
For fully two hours or three,
'Til Henry Martin gave to her the death shot, the death shot, the death shot,
Heavily listing to starboard went she.

The rich merchant vessel was wounded full sore,
And straight to the bottom went she,
And Henry Martin sailed away on the sea, salt sea, salt sea,
For to maintain his two brothers and he.

```
          Dm              C         Dm
Bad news, bad news to old England came,
               G           Dm A7
Bad news to fair London Town,
          Dm                              C7      F A7
There was a rich vessel and she's cast away, cast away, cast away,
     Bb F        C         Dm
And all of her merry men drowned.
```

Weel May the Keel Row

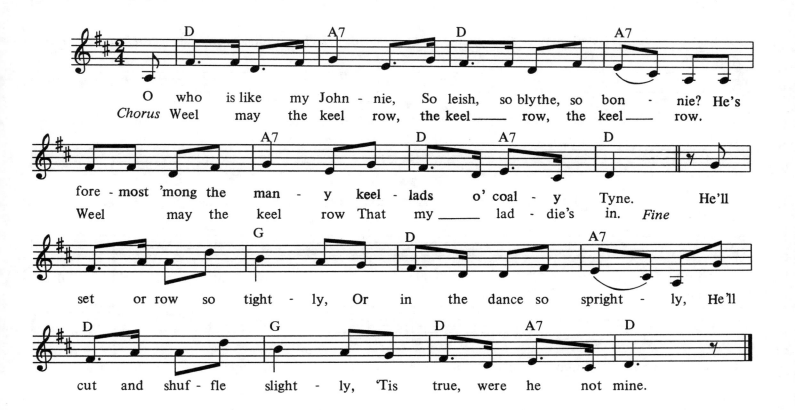

```
O who is like my John - nie, So leish, so blythe, so bon - nie? He's
Chorus Weel    may the keel  row,  the keel___ row, the keel___ row.

fore - most 'mong the man - y keel - lads o' coal - y Tyne.      He'll
Weel       may the keel row That my ___ lad - die's in. Fine

set   or row  so tight - ly, Or in  the dance so spright - ly, He'll

cut and shuf - fle slight - ly, 'Tis true, were he  not mine.
```

<table>
<tr><td>

```
     D         A7
He has nae mair o' learning,
     D         A7
Than tells his weekly earning,
     D         A7
Yet right frae wrang discerning,
     D         A7  D
Though brave, nae bruiser he.
          G
Though he's no worth a plack is
     D         A7
His ain coat on his back is,
     D         G
And nane can say that black is
     D      A7   D
The white o' Johnnie's e'e. Chorus
```

</td><td>

```
          D         A7
He wears a blue bonnet,
          D         A7
Blue bonnet, blue bonnet,
          D         A7
He wears a blue bonnet,
          D      A7   D
A dimple's in his chin.
               G
As I cam' thro' Sandgate,
          D         A7
Thro' Sandgate, thro' Sandgate,
          D         G
As I cam' thro' Sandgate
          D      A7   D
I heard a lassie sing: Chorus
```

</td></tr>
</table>

The Blantyre Explosion

The coal-rich parish of Blantyre lies a few miles southeast of Glasgow. Miners were bound into the occupation at birth. This form of serfdom, which lasted until almost the end of the 18th century, was accepted without protest. Mine owners could and did institute legal processes against miners who left their work. Needless to say, working and living conditions were abysmal. The disaster described in this song took place at the Dixon colliery in High Blantyre on October 22, 1877. Over 200 miners were killed.

"Twenty-one years of age, full of youth and good looking,
To work down the mines from High Blantyre he came.
The wedding was fixed, all the guests were invited;
That calm summer evening young Johnny was slain.
The explosion was heard, all the women and children,
With pale anxious faces, they haste to the mine.
When the truth was made known, the hills rang with their moaning;
Three hundred and ten young miners were slain."

Sung to first 15 measures.

Now husbands and wives and sweethearts and brothers,
That Blantyre explosion they'll never forget;
And all you young miners that hear my sad story,
Shed a tear for the victims who're laid to their rest."

26

The Bonnie Ship, the Diamond

Early in the 19th century, the Greenland Sea was fished nearly clean. Whalermen from Peterhead were attracted by the newly found grounds at the entrance to the Davis Strait (between Greenland and Canada) — the so-called Southwest Fishery. This song probably dates from the late 1820s. In 1830, one of the worst disasters of British whaling occurred when a large part of the fleet, including *The Diamond, The Resolution,* and the *Eliza Swan,* were locked in the far-northern ice of Melville Bay, Greenland. Twenty fine ships and scores of bold whalermen were lost.

Am   C
Along the quay at Peterhead,
  Am
The lasses stand around
               C
Wi' their shawls all pulled about them,
      E7   Am
And the saut tears rinnin' doon;
          C
Don't you weep, my bonnie lass,
    Am   Em
Though you be left behind,
    Am   C
For the rose will grow on Greenland's ice
 E7   Am
Before we change our mind. *Chorus*

                  Am   C
Here's a health to *The Resolution,*
           Am   Em
Likewise the *Eliza Swan,*
               Am   C
Here's a health to *The Battler of Montrose,*
           E7   Am
And *The Diamond,* ship of fame.
                        C
We wear the trousers of the white,
             Am   Em
And the jackets o' the blue,
            Am   C
When we return to Peterhead
        E7   Am
We'll ha'e sweethearts enoo. *Chorus*

         Am   C
It'll be bricht both day and nicht
           Am   Em
When the Greenland lads come hame,
           Am   C
Wi' a ship that's fu' o' oil, my lads,
        E7   Am
And money to our name;
                        C
We'll make the cradles for to rock
          Am   Em
And the blankets for to tear.
        Am   C
And every lass in Peterhead sing
   E7   Am
"Hushabye, my dear." *Chorus*

The Barnyards of Delgaty

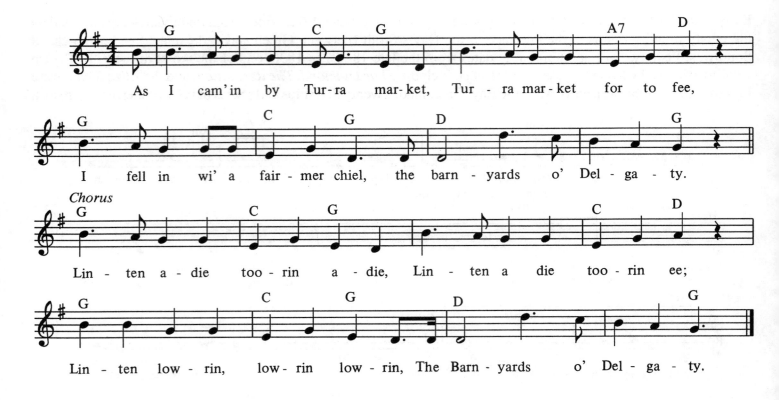

As I cam'in by Tur-ra mar-ket, Tur-ra mar-ket for to fee,

I fell in wi' a fair-mer chiel, the barn-yards o' Del-ga-ty.

Chorus

Lin - ten a-die too - rin a - die, Lin - ten a die too - rin ee;

Lin - ten low - rin, low - rin low - rin, The Barn - yards o' Del - ga - ty.

G   C   G
He promised me the ae best pair
           A7   D
That ever I set my e'en upon,
G   C   G
When I gaed to the Barnyards,
     D   G
There was naething there but skin and bone. *Chorus*

G   C   G
When I gae to the kirk on Sunday,
           A7   D
Mony's the bonnie lass I see,
G   C   G
Sitting by her father's side,
     D   G
And winkin' owre the pews at me. *Chorus*

G   C   G
The auld black horse sat on its rump,
           A7   D
The auld white mare lay on her wime,
G   C   G
And for a' that I could "Hup!" and crack,
   D   G
They wouldna rise at yokin' time. *Chorus*

G   C   G
I can drink and no' be drunk,
           A7   D
I can fecht and no' be slain,
G   C   G
I can lie wi' anither man's lass,
   D   G
And aye be welcome to my ain. *Chorus*

G   C   G
Noo my cannle is brunt oot,
               A7   D
My snotter's fairly on the wane,
      G   C   G
Sae fare ye weel, ye Barnyards,
     D   G
Ye'll never catch me here again! *Chorus*

chiel—young fellow   **fecht**—fight

Johnie Blunt

There liv'd a man in yon - der glen, And John Blunt was— his name, O; He maks — gude maut and he brews— gude ale, And he bears a won— drous fame, O.

| | E | B7 | E | B7 |
| The wind blew in the hallan ae night. |
| | E | A | E | B7 |
| Fu' snell out o'er the moor, O; |
| | E | A | E | B7 |
| "Rise up, rise up, auld Luckie," he says, |
| | E | A | B7 | E |
| "Rise up and bar the door, O." |

| | E | B7 | E | B7 |
| They made a paction tween them twa, |
| | E | A | E | B7 |
| They made it firm and sure, O, |
| | E | A | E | B7 |
| Whae'er sud speak the foremost word |
| | E | A | B7 | E |
| Should rise and bar the door, O. |

| | E | B7 | E | B7 |
| Three travellers that had tint their gate, |
| | E | A | E | B7 |
| As thro' the hills they foor, O, |
| | E | A | E | B7 |
| They airted by the line o' light |
| | E | A | B7 | E |
| Fu' straught to Johnie Blunt's door, O. |

| | E | B7 | E | B7 |
| They haurl'd auld Luckie out o' her bed, |
| | E | A | E | B7 |
| And laid her on the floor, O; |
| | E | A | E | B7 |
| But never a word auld Luckie wad say, |
| | E | A | B7 | E |
| For barrin o' the door, O. |

| | E | B7 | E | B7 |
| "Ye've eaten my bread, ye hae druken my ale, |
| | E | A | E | B7 |
| And ye'll mak my auld wife a whore, O." |
| | E | A | E | B7 |
| "Aha, Johnie Blunt! ye hae spoke the first word. |
| | E | A | B7 | E |
| Get up and bar the door, O." |

airted—took their direction
Blunt—Fool
foor—fared

hallan—partition between cottage door
　and fireplace
Luckie—wife

maut—malt
snell—bitter, keen
tint their gate—lost their way

29

The Work of the Weavers

By the 1780s the Industrial Revolution had arrived in Scotland. West Indian cotton became available in ever-increasing quantities. In 1792, the parish of Nielston possessed two cotton mills, employing more than 300 people (over half of them children) and 152 handlooms. The minister bemoaned this turn of events, for it engendered such outrageously expensive habits as tea and sugar for breakfast.

We're all met to-geth-er here, to sit and to crack. With our glass-es in our hands and our work up-on our back. And there's not a trade a-mong them all can ei-ther mend nor mak', If it was-na' for the work of the weav-ers. *Chorus* If it was-na' for the weav-ers what would they do? We would-na' have cloth made of our wool. We would-na' have a coat, nei-ther black nor blue, gin it was-na' for the work of the weav-ers.

The hireman chiels, they mock us, (G)
And crack aye aboot's. (C G)

They say we are thin-faced,
Bleached like cloots. (Am D7)

But yet for a' their mockery, (G)
They canna do wi' oots. (C G)

No! they canna want the work
Of the weavers. (D7 G) *Chorus*

There's our wrights and our slaters, (G)
And glaziers and a'. (C G)

Our doctors and our ministers,
And them that live by law; (Am D7)

And our friends in South America, (G)
Though them we never saw, (C G)

But we know they wear the work
Of the weavers. (D7 G) *Chorus*

cloots—clothes   **hireman chiels**—mill owners

                    G
There's our sailors and our soldiers,
        C   G
We know they're a' bold,

And if they hadna clothes, faith,
        Am   D7
They couldna live for cauld.
        G
The high and low, the rich and poor,
        C   G
A'body young and auld —

They winna want the work
        D7 G
Of the weavers.   *Chorus*

                    G
There's folk that's independent
        C   G
Of other tradesmen's work;

The women need no barbers,
        Am   D7
And dykers need no clerk;
        G
But none of them can do without
        C   G
A coat or a shirt.

No! they canna want the work
        D7 G
Of the weavers.   *Chorus*

                    G
The weaving is a trade
        C   G
That can never fail,

As long's we need a cloth
        Am   D7
To keep another hale;
        G
So let us aye be merry
        C   G
Over a bicker of good ale,

And drink to the health
        D7 G
Of the weavers.   *Chorus*

Maiden of the Dark Brown Hair

The Hebrides

Chorus Dm — C — Dm — Gm — F
Maid - en   of   the dark brown hair,   Far   with her   I'd wan - der,__

Dm — C — Dm — *Verse* Gm — Dm — Am
Maid-en   of   the dark brown hair. Long   have I   been wait-ing here   A - lone   and full of   sor - row.__
Fine

Gm
I outside behind the house remain
     Dm   Am
While you inside are courting.   *Chorus*

Gm
East and west I'd walk with you
     Dm   Am
Without my horse and bridle.   *Chorus*

Gm
Through the Sound of Mull I'd go,
     Dm   Am
Nor wait to put my shoes on.   *Chorus*

Gm
To Kintyre I'd go with you,
     Dm   Am
Where I was well acquainted.   *Chorus*

Gm
I would go to Uist with you,
     Dm   Am
Where barley ripens golden.   *Chorus*

Gm
I would reach the stars with you,
     Dm   Am
If your own folk were willing. *Chorus*

Gm
I would reach the moon with you,
     Dm   Am
If you would say we'll marry.   *Chorus*

31

Jamie Raeburn's Farewell

Jamie, and thousands of other Scottish, Irish and English convicts like him were "transported" to Botany Bay. Jamie's one-way voyage took place in 1814. He was accused of simple theft, which he denied — but to no avail.

My name is Ja-mie Rae-burn, ___ in Glas-gow I was born. ___ My place and ha - bi - ta-tion ___ I'm forced to leave with scorn. ___ From my place and ha - bi - ta-tion ___ I noo must gang a wa; ___ Far frae the bon-nie hills and dales of Ca - le - do - ni - a. ___

G   Em   C   G
It was early one morning just by the break of day,
      Am   G   Am   D
We were wakened by the turnkey, who unto us did say,
      C   Bm   Am   G
"Arise, ye hapless convicts, arise ye ane and a',
      Bm   Em   C   G
This is the day ye are to stray from Caledonia."

G   Em   C   G
We a' arose, put on oor claes, oor hearts were fu' o' grief,
        Am   G   Am   D
Oor friends, wha stood round the coach, could grant us no relief;
      C   Bm   Am   G
Oor parents, wives and sweethearts dear, their hearts were broke in twa,
      Bm   Em   C   G
To see us leave the bonnie braes o' Caledonia.

G   Em   C   G
Farewell, my aged mither, I'm vexed for what I've done,
Am   G   Am   D
I hope nane will cast up to you the race that I have run;
      C   Bm   Am   G
I hope God will protect you when I am far awa',
      Bm   Em   C   G
Far frae the bonnie hills and dales o' Caledonia.

Bonnie George Campbell

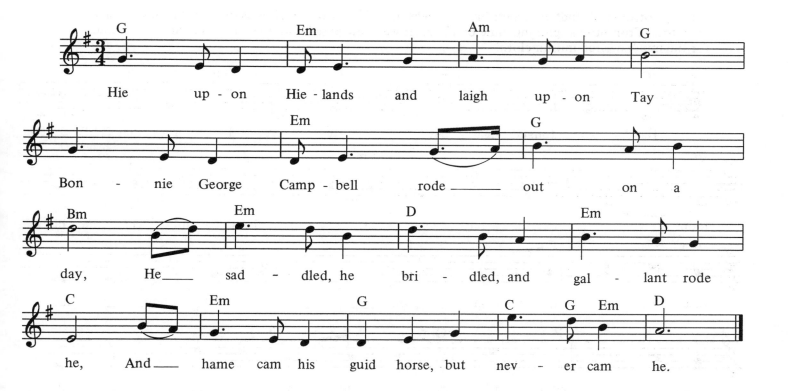

Hie up - on Hie - lands and laigh up - on Tay

Bon - nie George Camp - bell rode ____ out on a

day, He ____ sad - dled, he bri - dled, and gal - lant rode

he, And ____ hame cam his guid horse, but nev - er cam he.

```
G       Em        Am      G
Out cam his mother dear, greeting fu' sair,
              Em        G       Bm
And out cam his bonnie bride, riving her hair.
      Em      D      Em        C
The meadow lies green, the corn is unshorn,
      Em        G       C G Em D
But bonnie George Campbell will never return.


G       Em        Am      G
Saddled and bridled and booted rode he,
              Em      G       Bm
A plume in his helmet, a sword at his knee.
      Em        D      Em        C
But toom cam his saddle, all bloody to see,
      Em      G       C G Em D
Oh, hame cam his guid horse, but never cam he!
```

toom—empty

Haud Yer Tongue Dear Sally

The big cotton mills that were built in the 1780s and 1790s owed their existence to the new English invention, Crompton's spinning mule of 1779. It was now possible to mass produce the fine threads for the much-desired muslin cloth.

Haud yer tongue dear Sal - ly ere I gae tae the toon._____ I'll buy tae ye_____ a jaunt - in' car and like - wise a mu - za - lin goon,_____ I'll buy_____ tae ye_____ a jaunt - in' car_____ and a braw_____ white mu - za - lin goon. _____ Like___ wise a lit - tle wee lap_____ dog to fol - low your jaunt - in' car._____

| | C | | F C | Dm | F | C | | | C | | F C | Dm | F | C |
The De'il gae wi' yer lapdog, yer jauntin' car and a'. / For your pipes is never in order, your chanter it's never in tune.

| | Em | F | G | | Am | C | G |
I wisht I had a young man with never a penny ava. / I wisht the Devil had you and a young man in your room,

| | C | | F | G | | Am | C | G G7 |
I wisht I had a young man with never a penny ava, / I wisht the Devil had you and a young man in your room,

| | C | | F | C Am | F | | C |
But I had just gotten an old man to roll me tae the wall. / I'd rather have a young man with ne'er a penny ava.

| | C | | F | C | Dm | F | | C |
It's noo she's gotten a young man with ne'er a penny ava,

| | C | | Em | F | G | | Am | C | G |
It's noo she's gotten her young man to roll her tae the wa'.

| | C | | F | G | | Am | C | G G7 |
He broke her china cups and saucers, he lay and broke them all,

| | C | | F | C Am | F | | C |
And he kill't her little wee lapdog that followed her jauntin' car.

a'—all   **De'il**—Devil   **goon**—gown   **muzalin**—muslin   **tae**—to   **wa'**—wall
ava—at all   **gae**—go   **haud**—hold   **noo**—now   **toon**—town

O, Are Ye Sleepin', Maggie?

Mirk and rain-y is the nicht, There's no a star— in a' the car-ry,— Light-ning gleams a-cross the sky, And winds they blaw— wi' win-ter fu-ry,—

Chorus

And it's o, are— ye— sleep-in' Mag-gie? O, are— ye— sleep-in' Mag-gie?— Let me in, for loud the linn is roor-in' ow-er the— war-lock's Crai-gie.

Em Am Em Am
Fearfu' soughs the boortree bank,
Em D C Em
The rifted wood roars wild and dreary,
Am Em Am
Loud the iron yett does clank,
Em D C Em
And cry o' howlets mak me eerie. *Chorus*

Em Am Em Am
Aboon my breath I daurna speak
Em D C Em
For fear I'll rouse your wakefu' daddie
Am Em Am
Cauld's the blast upon my cheek,
Em D C Em
O rise, O rise, my bonnie lassie. *Chorus*

Em Am Em Am
She's op'ed the door, she's let him in,
Em D C Em
He's cuist aside his dreeping plaidie.
Am Em Am
"Ye can blaw your worst, ye winds and rain
Em D C Em
Since, Maggie, noo I'm in aside ye!"

Final Chorus:

Am G
O, noo that ye're waukin' Maggie
D G
O, noo that ye're waukin' Maggie
Em Am D
What care I, for howlets cry,
Em D Em
For roarin' linn or warlock's cragie?

aboon—above
boortree—elder tree, shrub
carry—the heavens
cuist—cast, thrown aside
daurna—dare not

dreeping—soaking wet
howlets—owls
linn—waterfall
mirk—dark
plaidie—plaid, rough cloak

soughs—sighs
warlock's craigie—wizard's crag
waukin'—awake
yett—gate

Maids, When You're Young Never Wed an Old Man

". . . And as for adulterie, fornicatioun, incest, bigamie, and uther uncleanes and filthynes, it did never abound moir nor at this tyme." (From the diary of James Nicolls, Edinburgh, 1650)

E
Now, when we went to church,
      B7
Hey ding doorum down,
E
Now, when we went to church,
      B7
Hey doorum down;
  E   B7
When we went to church,
E   B7
He left me in the lurch.
  E   A   B7   E
Maids, when you're young, never wed an old man. *Chorus*

E
Now, when we went to bed,
      B7
Hey, ding doorum down,
E
Now, when we went to bed,
      B7
Hey, doorum down;
       E   B7
Now, when we went to bed
E   B7
He neither done nor said.
  E   A   B7
Maids, when you're young, never wed and old man. *Chorus*

            E
Now, when he went to sleep,
      B7
Hey ding doorum down,
      E   B7
Now, when he went to sleep,
      B7
Hey doorum down;
      E   B7
Now, when he went to sleep,
   E   B7
Out of bed I did creep,
  E   A   B7   E
Into the arms of a jolly young man.

Final Chorus:
        E   B7
And I found his fal-looral fal-liddle fal-looral,
E   B7
I found his fal-looral, fal-liddle all day,
  E   B7   E   B7
I found his fal-loorum and he got my ding doorum,
      E   A   B7   E
So maids, when you're young, never wed an old man.

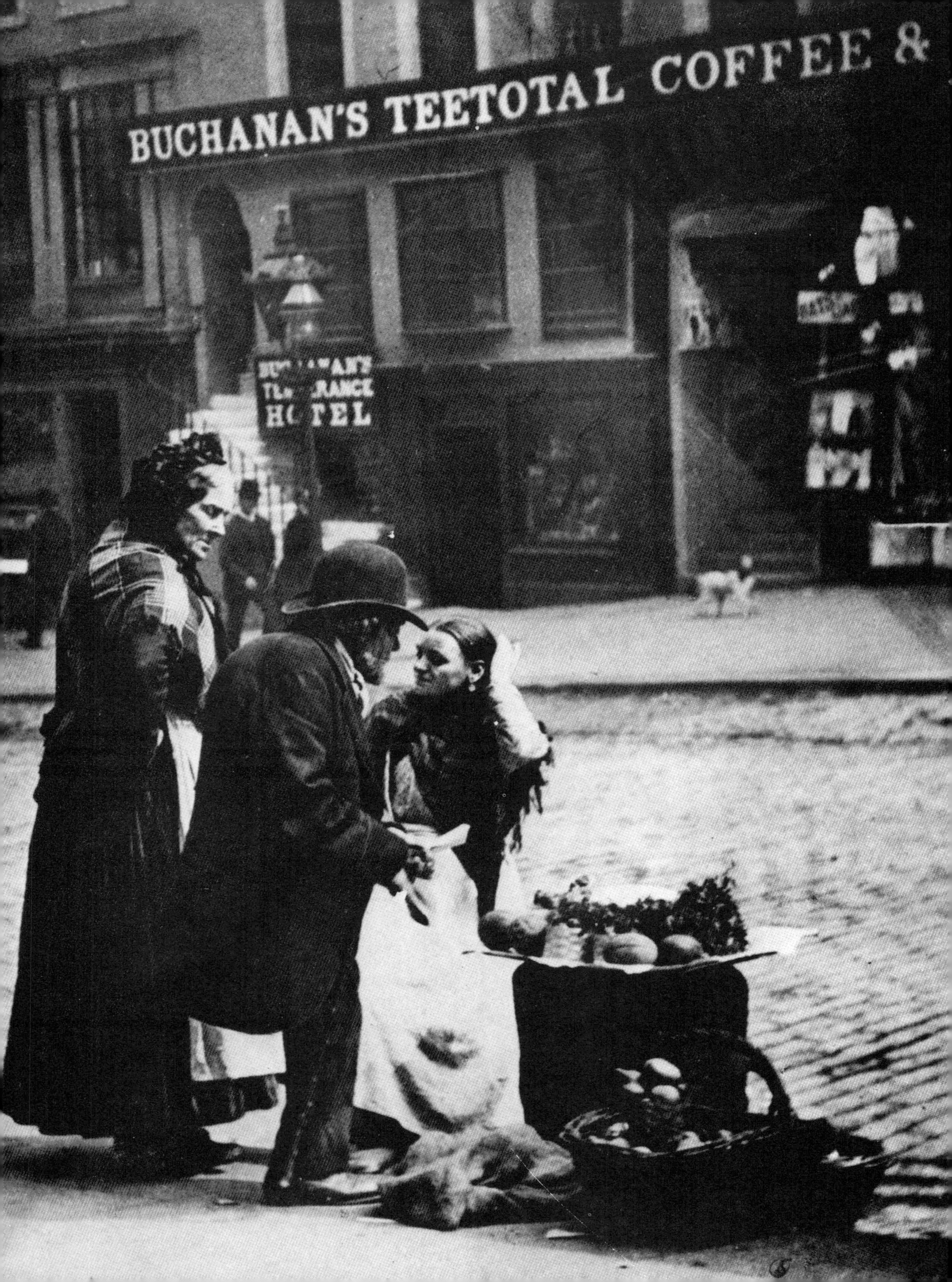
BUCHANAN'S TEETOTAL COFFEE &
HOTEL

Rigs o' Rye

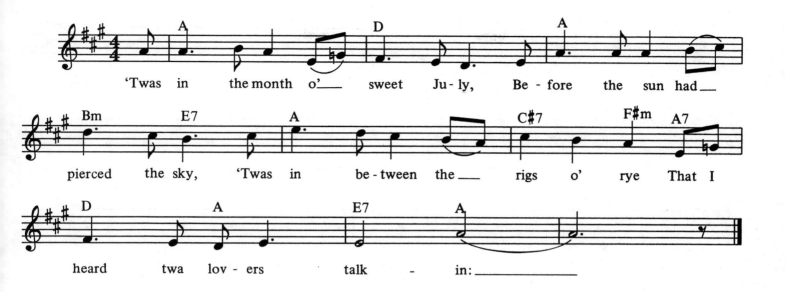

'Twas in the month o'— sweet Ju-ly, Be-fore the sun had—
pierced the sky, 'Twas in be-tween the — rigs o' rye That I
heard twa lov-ers talk - in: _____

A   D
The lad said, "Lassie, I must away,
   A   Bm   E7
I have no longer time tae stay
   A   C#7   F#m
But I've a word or two tae say,
A7 D   A   E7 A
If you've got time tae tarry.

    A   D
Your father of you he taks great care,
   A   Bm E7
Your mother combs doon your yellow hair.
    A   C#7   F#m
Your sisters say that you'll get nae share.
A7   D   A   E7 A
If you gang wi' me, a stranger."

     A   D
"Let my faither fret and my mither frown,
   A   Bm E7
My sisters' words I do disown
    A   C#7   F#m
Tho' they were deid and below the grun,
A7   D   A   E7 A
I would gang wi' you, a stranger."

    A   D
"O lassie, lassie, your fortune's sma'
   A   Bm E7
And maybe it will be nane ava,
    A   C#7   F#m
You're no' a match for me at a;
A7 D   A   E7 A
Lay ye your love on some other."

    A   D
The lassie's courage began tae fail,
   A   Bm   E7
Her rosy cheeks they grew wan and pale,
     A   C#7   F#m
And the tears cam trinklin' doon like hail,
A7 D   A   E7 A
Or a heavy shower in summer.

    A   D
But he's ta'en his hankercher linen fine,
    A   Bm   E7
He's dried her tears and he's kissed her, syne,
    A   C#7   F#m
Sayin', "Lassie, lassie, ye shall be mine,
A7 D   A   E7 A
I said it a' just tae try ye."

    A   D
This laddie bein' o' courage bold
   A   Bm   E7
A bonnie lad, scarce nineteen year old,
    A   C#7   F#m
He's ranged the hills and the valleys ower,
A7   D   A   E7 A
And he's ta'en his lassie wi' him.

    A   D
And, aye, this couple are mairrit noo,
   A   Bm   E7
And they hae bairnies one and two,
    A   C#7   F#m
And they live in Brechin the winter through,
A7 D   A   E7 A
And in Montrose in summer.

The Pride of Glencoe

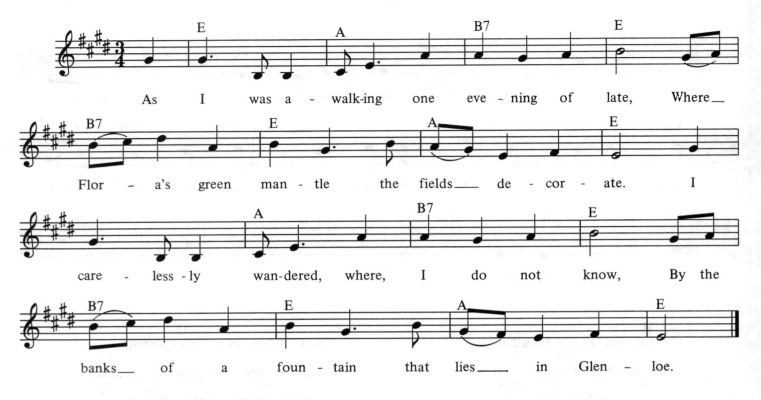

As I was a-walk-ing one eve-ning of late, Where Flor-a's green man-tle the fields de-cor-ate. I care-less-ly wan-dered, where, I do not know, By the banks of a foun-tain that lies in Glen-loe.

E   A   B7   E
Like she who the pride of Mount lda had won,
B7   E   A   E
There approached a wee lassie as fair as the sun,
A   B7   E
With ribbons and tartans around her did flow,
B7   E   A   E
That once won MacDonald, the pride of Glencoe.

E   A   B7   E
With courage undaunted, I to her drew nigh,
B7   E   A   E
While the red rose and lily on her cheek seemed to vie.
A   B7   E
I asked her her name and how far she did go,
B7   E   A   E
And she answered, "Be kind, sir, I'm bound for Glencoe."

E   A   B7   E
I said, "My wee lassie, your enchanting smile
B7   E   A   E
And your comely fine features have my heart beguiled.
A   B7   E
If your kind affections on me you'll bestow,
B7   E   A   E
I will bless the happy hour we met in Glencoe."

E   A   B7   E
"Kind sir," she made answer, "your suit I disdain,
B7   E   A   E
I once had a sweetheart, MacDonald by name,
A   B7   E
He's gone to the war about ten years ago,
B7   E   A   E
And a maid I'll remain till he returns to Glencoe."

E   A   B7   E
"Perhaps young MacDonald regards not your name,
B7   E   A   E
And has placed his affection on some other dame.
A   E
Perhaps he's forgotten for all that you know,
B7   E   A   E
The bonnie wee lassie he left in Glencoe."

E   A   B7   E
"My Donald from his promise will never depart,
B7   E   A   E
For love, truth and honour are found in his heart.
A   B7   E
And if I never see him, I single will go,
B7   E   A   E
And I'll mourn for my Donald, the pride of Glencoe."

E   A   B7   E
He finding her constant, he pulled out a glove,
B7   E   A   E
Which at parting she gave him as a token of love.
A   B7   E
She flew to his arms while the tears down did flow,
B7   E   A
Saying, "You're welcome, my Donald, the pride of Glenc

E   A   B7   E
"Cheer up, now young Flora, your sorrows are o'er,
B7   E   A   E
And while life still remains we will never part more.
B7   E
The storms of war at a distance may blow,
B7   E   A   E
While in peace and contentment we'll bide in Glencoe."

Sir Patrick Spens

In 1266 Norway agreed to renounce all claims to the Hebrides. It was also stipulated in the treaty that Margaret, daughter of Scottish King Alexander III, should be betrothed to Eric, son of King Magnus of Norway. The marriage took place in 1281. The young queen had to be conducted to Norway. On the return trip a terrible storm arose, and many of the Scottish nobles who had escorted her were drowned.

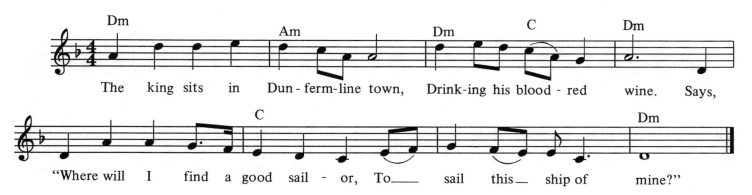

The king sits in Dunfermline town, Drinking his blood-red wine. Says, "Where will I find a good sailor, To sail this ship of mine?"

Dm   Am
Then up spoke an elder knight,
Dm C Dm
He sat at the king's right knee:
      C
"Sir Patrick Spens is the best sailor,
     Dm
That ever sailed the sea."

Dm   Am
The king has written a broad letter,
Dm C Dm
And signed it with his hand,
      C
And sent it to Sir Patrick Spens,
     Dm
Who was walking on the sand.

Dm   Am
The first line Sir Patrick read,
Dm C Dm
A loud laugh laughed he;
      C
The second line Sir Patrick read,
     Dm
The tears they blinded his eye.

  Dm   Am
To Norrowa', to Norriwa',
  D C Dm
To Norrowa', ower the faem;
      C
The King's dochter to Norrowa',
      Dm
Tis ye mun bring her hame.

  Dm   Am
"Oh, who is this, has done this thing,
Dm C Dm
To tell the king of me?
      C
And send me out this time of year,
      Dm
On such a wint'ry sea?

  Dm   Am
"Make haste, make haste, my merry men all,
  Dm C Dm
Our good ship sails in the morn."
      C
"Oh, don't say that, my captain dear,
      Dm
For I fear a deadly storm."

  Dm   Am
"Last night I saw the new moon,
  Dm C Dm
With the old moon in her arms;
      C
Oh, let's not sail, my captain dear,
      Dm
For I fear we'll come to harm."

  Dm   Am
Now, loath, loath were our good Scots Lords
  Dm C Dm
To wet their cork-heeled shoon,
      C
But ere the game were half played out,
      Dm
Their hats they swam aboon.

  Dm   Am
And long, long may their ladies sit
  Dm C Dm
With their fans in their hands,
      C
Before they see Sir Patrick Spens
      Dm
Come sailing back to land.

  Dm   Am
Half o'er, half o'er to Aberdour
  Dm C Dm
It's fifty fathoms deep,
      C
And there lies good Sir Patrick Spens,
      Dm
With the Scots Lords at his feet.

To the Begging I Will Go

During the famine of the 1690s, it has been estimated that one-sixth of the population of Scotland — anywhere from 150,000 to 200,000 people — were begging. Some suggested at the time that this displaced mass be transported overseas to found colonies.

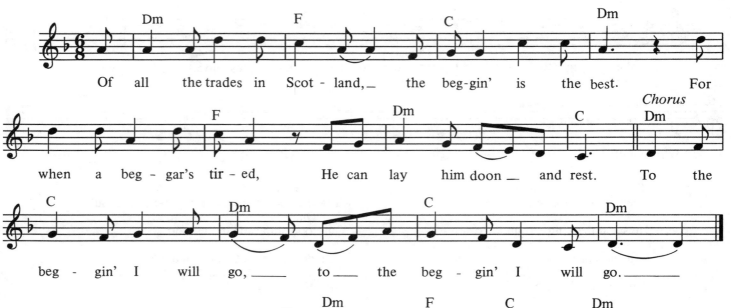

Of all the trades in Scot-land,— the beg-gin' is the best. For when a beg-gar's tir-ed, He can lay him doon — and rest. *Chorus* To the beg-gin' I will go, _____ to __ the beg-gin' I will go. _____

Dm F C Dm
I've a pocket for my oatmeal, and another for my salt.
 F Dm C
I've a pair of little crutches, you should see how I can halt. *Chorus*

Dm F C Dm
There's patches on me dusty coat, and another for me ee;
 F Dm C
But when it comes to tup'ny ale, I can see as well as thee. *Chorus*

Dm F C Dm
My britches, they are nowt but holes, but my heart is free from care,
 F Dm C
As long as I've my belly full, my backside can go bare. *Chorus*

Dm F C Dm
I've been deaf in Dumfries, and I've been blind at Awe,
 F Dm C
But many's the right and willing lass, I've bedded in the straw. *Chorus*

Dm F C Dm
I can rest my head where e're I choose, and I don't pay no rent,
 F Dm C
I've got no noisy loons to mind, and I am right content. *Chorus*

Dm F C Dm
I can rest when I am tired, and I heed no master's bell,
 F Dm C
A man 'ud be daft to be a king, when beggars live so well. *Chorus*

loons—rascals

The Wee Wee Man

As I ___ was walk - ing all ___ a-lone ___ be-tween ___ a wa - ter and ___ a wa,' And
there ___ I spyed ___ a wee ___ wee man, And he was the least ___ that ere ___ I saw. His ___
legs were scarce a shath - mont's length ___ And thick and thim - ber was ___ his thigh, ___ Be -
tween his brows there was ___ a span, And be-tween ___ his shoul - ders there ___ was three.

Am
He took up a meikle stane,
G
And he flang't as far as I could see;
Am   Dm
Tho I had been a Wallace wight
Am   G
I couldna liften't to my knee.
C   Am
"O wee wee man but thou be strong,
C   Dm
O tell me whare thy dwelling be."
C   Am   Dm
"My dwelling's down at yon bonny bower,
Am   G
O will you go with me and see?"

Am
On we lap and awa we rade,
G
Till we came to yon bonny green;
Am   Dm
We lighted down for to bait our horse,
Am   G
And out there came a lady fine.
C   Am
Four and twenty at her back,
C   Dm
And they were a' clad out in green;
C   Am   Dm
Tho the king of Scotland had been there,
Am   G
The warst o' them might hae been his queen.

Am
On we lap and awa we rade,
G
Till we cam to yon bonny ha',
Am   Dm
Whare the roof was o' the beaten gould
Am   G
And the floor was o' crista'.
C   Am
When we came to the stair foot,
C   Dm
Ladies were dancing jimp and sma,
C   Am   Dm
But in the twinkling of an eye,
Am   G
My wee wee man was clean awa.

bait—rest and feed
jimp—graceful
lap—leaped
meikle—large
shathmont—measurement from the tip of the
   outstretched thumb across the palm (six inches)
sma—slender
span—measurement of the extended hand (nine inches)
thimber—massive
wa'—wall
a Wallace wight—as strong as Wallace himself

Son David

I recorded this from the singing of the great traditional ballad singer Jeannie Robertson in her home in Aberdeen in June 1959.

O,___ what's the blood 'at's on your sword, My son Da - vid, ho, son Da - vid?

What's that blood 'at's on ___ your sword? Come prom-ise, tell me ___ true.

G
O that's the blood of my grey meir,
Em
Hey, lady mother, ho, lady mother;
G   Em
That's the blood of my grey meir,
        G   C   G
Because it wadnae rule by me.

G
O that blood it is owre clear,
Em
My son David, ho, son David,
G   Em
That blood it is owre clear;
        G   C   G
Come promise, tell me true.

G
O that's the blood of my grey hound,
Em
Hey, lady mother, ho, lady mother;
G   Em
That's the blood of my grey hound,
        G   C   G
Because it wadnae rule by me.

G
O that blood it is owre clear,
Em
My son David, ho, son David,
G   Em
That blood it is owre clear;
        G   C   G
Come promise, tell me true.

G
O that's the blood of my huntin' hawk,
Em
Hey, lady mother, ho, lady mother;
G   Em
That's the blood of my huntin' hawk,
        G   C   G
Because it wadnae rule by me.

G
O that blood it is owre clear,
Em
My son David, ho, son David;
G   Em
That blood it is owre clear;
        G   C   G
Come promise, tell me true.

G
For that's the blood of my brother John,
Em
Hey, lady mother, ho, lady mother;
G   Em
That's the blood of my brother John,
        G   C   G
Because he wadnae rule by me.

G
O I'm gaun awa' in a bottomless boat,
Em
In a bottomless boat, in a bottomless boat,
G   Em
For I'm gaun awa' in a bottomless boat,
        G   C   G
An I'll never return again.

G
O whan will you come back again,
Em
My son David, ho, son David?
G   Em
Whan will you come back again?
        G   C G
Come promise, tell true.

G
When the sun an' the moon meet in yon glen,
Em
Hey, lady mother, ho, lady mother;
G   Em
Whan the sun an' the moon meet in yon glen,
        G   C   G
'Fore I'll return again.

owre—too   **wadnae rule**—would not be controlled

The Gypsy Rover

The tale of the "high-born" lady who gives up everything to follow her gypsy lover is well known in many versions throughout the British Isles and the United States. In some instances she leaves to follow Gypsy Davy or Johnny Faa. Sometimes he is merely identified as "the whistling gypsy."

The gyp-sy ro-ver come o-ver the hill, Bound through the val-ley so shad-y; He whis-tled and he sang till the green woods rang, And he won the heart of a la - dy._____ —

Chorus (same music as verse)

```
G    D7    G    D7
Ah di do, ah di do da day,
G    C    G    D7
Ah di do, ah di day dee.
G         D7    G    Em
He whistled and he sang till the green woods rang,
G     C      G C G (D7)
And he won the heart of a la-a-a-dy. last time no D7
```

```
      G      D7  G   D7
She left her father's castle gate,
   G       C     G D7
She left her own true lover.
   G        D7      G Em
She left her servants and her estate,
G       C    G C  G D7
To follow the gypsy ro-o-o - ver. Chorus
```

```
       G D7       G     D7
Her father saddled his fastest steed,
G       C      G D7
Roamed the valley all over.
 G         D7     G     Em
Sought his daughter at great speed,
    G       C    G C    G D7
And the whistling gypsy ro-o-o - ver. Chorus
```

```
      G     D7     G     D7
He came at last to a mansion fine,
C         C   G   D7
Down by the River Claydie.
      G       D7     G    Em
And there was music and there was wine,
        G    C    G   C G D7
For the gypsy and his la-a-a-dy.   Chorus
```

```
     G        D7     G      D7
"He's no gypsy, my father," said she, ,
       G   C        G D7
"My lord of freelands all over,
   G      D7     G    Em
And I will stay till my dying day
          G    C   G  C   G D7
With my whistling gypsy ro-o-o - ver." Chorus
```

Lord Randal

"Where have you been all the day, Ran-dal, my son? Where have you been all the day, my pret-ty one?" "I've been to my sweet-heart's, moth-er, __ I've been to my sweet-heart's moth-er. __ Make my bed soon, for I'm sick to my heart, and I fain would lie down."

C
"What have you been eating there, Randal, my son?
G
What have you been eating there, my pretty one?"
Am   Em
"Eels and eelbroth, mother,
Am   Em   G7
Eels and eelbroth, mother." *Chorus*

C
"Where did she get them from, Randal, my son?
G
Where did she get them from, my pretty one?"
Am   Em
"From hedges and ditches, mother,
Am   Em   G7
From hedges and ditches, mother." *Chorus*

C
"What was the color of their skin, Randal, my son?
G
What was the color of their skins, my pretty one?"
Am   Em
"Spickle and sparkle, mother,
Am   Em   G7
Spickle and sparkle, mother." *Chorus*

C
"I fear you are poisoned, Randal, my son,
G
I fear you are poisoned, my handsome young one."
Am   Em
"O yes, I'm poisoned, mother,
Am   Em G7
O yes, I'm poisoned, mother." *Chorus*

C
"What will you leave your father, Randal, my son?
G
What will you leave your father, my handsome young one?"
Am   Em
"My land and houses, mother,
Am   Em   G7
My land and houses, mother." *Chorus*

      C
"What will you leave your mother, Randal, my son?
                                      G
What will you leave your mother, my handsome young one?"
    Am   Em
"My gold and silver, mother ,
    Am   Em   G7
My gold and silver, mother." *Chorus*

      C
"What will you leave your brother, Randal, my son?
                                     G
What will you leave your brother, my handsome young one?"
    Am   Em
"My cows and horses, mother,
    Am   Em   G7
My cows and horses, mother." *Chorus*

       C
"What will you leave your sister, Randal, my son?
                                G
What will you leave your sister, my handsome young one?"
    Am   Em
"My box of gold rings, mother,
    Am   Em   G7
My box of gold rings, mother." *Chorus*

    C
"What will you leave your sweetheart, Randal, my son?
                                 G
What will you leave your sweetheart, my handsome young one?"
    Am   Em
"A rope to hang her, mother,
  Am   Em   G7
A rope to hang her, mother." *Chorus*

The Bonnie House o' Airlie

In June 1640, Archibald Campbell, lst marquess and 8th earl of Argyll, having been entrusted by the Scottish Parliament with a "commission of fire and sword" against the royalists in Atholl and Angus, which he carried out with completeness and some cruelty, set upon and burned "the bonnie house o' Airlie".

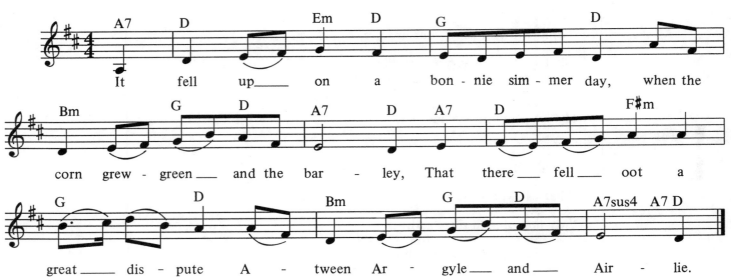

A7 D   Em D G   D
Argyle he has chosen a hundred o' his men,
  Bm   G D A7 D
He marched them out right early;
A7 D   F♯m   G   D
He led them doon by the back o' Dunkeld
  Bm   G   D   A7sus4 A7 D
To plunder the bonnie house o' Air ——— lie.

A7 D   Em D G   D
The Lady looked owre her window sae hie,
  Bm   G D A7 D
And oh but she grat sairly
A7 D F♯m G   D
To see Argyle and a' his men
  Bm   G   D   A7sus4 A7 D
Come to plunder the bonnie house o' Air ——— lie.

A7 D   Em D G   D
"Come doon, come doon, Lady Ogilvie," he cried,
   Bm   G D A7 D
"Come doon and kiss me fairly,
A7 D F♯m   G
Or I swear by the hilt o" my good broad sword
  Bm   G   D   A7sus4 A7 D
That I winna leave a stanin' stane in Air ——— lie."

A7 D   Em D G D
"I winna come down, ye cruel Argyle,
  Bm G D A7 D
I winna kiss ye fairly;
A7 D F♯m G   D
I wadna kiss ye, fause Argyle,
   Bm   G   D   A7sus4 A7 D
Tho' ye sudna leave a stanin' stane in Air ——— lie."

A7 D   Em D G D
"Come tell me where your dowry is hid,
   Bm G D A7 D
Come tell it to me fairly,
 A7 D F♯m   G   D
Come tell me where your dowry is hid,
   Bm   G   D   A7sus4 A7 D
Or I winna leave a stanin' stane in Air ——— lie."

A7 D Em D G   D
"I winna tell ye, fause Argyle,
  Bm G D A7 D
I winna tell ye fairly,
A7 D F♯m   G   D
I winna tell ye where my dowry is hid,
   Bm   G   D A7sus4 A7 D
Tho' ye sudna leave a stanin' stane in Air ——— lie."

A7 D   Em D G   D
So they sought up, and they sought down,
  Bm   G D A7 D
I wat they sought it sairly,
A7 D   F♯m   G   D
And it was below the bowling green
    Bm   G D A7sus4 A7 D
They found the dowry of Air ——— lie.

A7 D   Em D G   D
"Gin my good lord had been at hame,
  Bm G D   A7 D
As he's awa' wi' Charlie,
A7 D F♯m G   D
There durstna a Campbell o' a Argyle
  Bm   G D   A7sus4 A7 D
Set a fit on the bonnie green o' Air ——— lie."

```
    A7 D   Em D  G   D
"Eleven bairns hae I born,
        Bm       G   D  A7 D
And the twelfth ne'er saw his daddy;
 A7 D      F♯m    G    D
But though I had gotten as mony again
      Bm    G      D       A7sus4  A7   D
They sud a' gang to fecht for Char ——— lie."


    A7  D   Em D  G    D
"But since it's so, tak ye my hand,
      Bm   G   D  A7 D
And see ye lead me fairly;
 A7 D     F♯m   G    D
Ye lead me doon to yonder glen,
      Bm        G  D    A7sus4  A7  D
That I mayna see the burnin' o' Air ——— lie."
```

```
    A7 D      Em D  G      D
He's ta'en her by the milk-white hand,
      Bm   G   D  A7 D
But he didna lead her fairly;
 A7 D    F♯m    G       D
He led her up to the tap o' the hill,
        Bm    G   D    A7sus4  A7  D
Where she saw the burnin' o' Air ——— lie.


    A7  D      Em D   G     D
The smoke and the flames they rose sae hie,
      Bm       G  D    A7 D
The walls were blackened fairly,
 A7       D      F♯m      G       D
And the Lady laid her down on the green to die,
        Bm    G   D    A7sus4  A7  D
When she saw the burnin' o' Air ——— lie.
```

Charlie—Charles I   **grat**—wept   **stanin' stane**—standing stone
Gin—If   **house of Airlie**—west of Forfar   **wat**—know

Brown Adam, the Smith

O wha wou'd wish the win' to blaw, or the green leaves fa' there-
with; Or wha wou'd wish a tru-er love than Brown Ad-am, the smith?

Am   C   Em Am
His hammer's o' the beaten gold,
   C   Am   G
His study's o' the steel,
   Am   C   Em C
His fingers white are my delite,
  Am   Em   Am
He blows his bellows weel.

    Am   C   Em   Am
But they ha' banish'd Brown Adam
    C   Am   G
Frae father and frae mither,
    Am   C   Em   C
An' they ha' banish'd Brown Adam
  Am Em   Am
Frae sister and frae brither.

    Am   C   Em   Am
And they ha' banish'd Brown Adam
    C   Am   G
Frae the flow'r o' a' his kin;
    Am   C   Em   C
An' he's bigget a bow'r i' the good green wood
  Am   Em   Am
Between his lady an' him.

  Am   C   Em Am
O, it fell once upon a day,
   C Am   G
Brown Adam he thought lang,
   Am   C   Em   C
An' he wou'd to the green wood gang
  Am   Em Am
To hunt some venison.

   Am   C   Em Am
He's ta'en his bow his arm o'er,
   C Am   G
His bran' intill his han',
   Am C   Em   C
And he is to the good green wood
  Am   Em   Am
As fast as he cou'd gang.

   Am   C   Em   Am
O, he's shot up an' he's shot down
    C Am   G
The bird upo' the briar,
    Am   C   Em   C
An' he's sent it hame to his lady,
    Am Em   Am
Bade her be of good cheer.

   Am   C   Em   Am
O, he's shot up an' he's shot down,
    C Am   G
The bird upo' the thorn,
   Am   C   Em   C
And sent it hame to his lady,
   Am Em   Am
And he'd be hame the morn.

    Am   C   Em   Am
Whan he came till his lady's bow'r-door,
    C Am   G
He stood a little foreby;
   Am   C   Em   C
And there he heard a fu' fa'se knight
  Am   Em   Am
Temptin' his gay lady.

   Am   C   Em   Am
O, he's ta'en out a gay gold ring,
    C Am   G
Had cost him mony a poun':
   Am   C   Em   C
"O, grant me love for love, lady,
    Am Em   Am
An' this sal be your own."

   Am   C   Em   Am
"I loo' Brown Adam well," she says,
    C Am   G
"I wot sae does he me,
   Am   C   Em   C
An' I wou'd na gi' Brown Adam's love
  Am   Em   Am
For nae fa'se knight I see."

bigget—built
bran' intill—sword into
foreby—aside
gang—go

gar'd—forced . . . to
light leman—whore
mair nor—more than

the morn—on the morrow
thought lang—grew bored
wot—know

```
  Am      C    Em    Am                          Am        C      Em       Am
Out has he ta'en a purse of gold,             Then out has he drawn his lang, lang bran;
    C    Am   G                                   C            Am    G
Was a' fu' to the string:                     And he's flash'd it in her e'en:
       Am     C      Em      C                      Am      C      Em      C
"Grant me but love for love, lady,            "Now grant me love for love, lady,
    Am    Em    Am                                Am    Em       Am
An' a' this sal be thine."                    Or thro' you this sal gang."


  Am      C    Em    Am                           Am   C   Em   Am
"I loo Brown Adam well," she says,            O, sighing said that gay lady,
      C       Am   G                                 C       Am    G
"An' I ken sae does he me,                    "Brown Adam tarrys lang";
       Am      C     Em    C                      Am     C        Em  C
An' I wou'dna be your light leman             Then up it starts Brown Adam,
      Am    Em    Am                              Am     Em      Am
For mair nor ye cou'd gie."                   Says, "I'm just at your han'."


                      Am       C     Em     Am
                    He's gar'd him leave his bow, his bow,
                       C      Am        G
                    He's gar'd him leave his bran';
                       Am       C    Em       C
                    He's gar'd him leave a better pledge,
                          Am    Em      Am
                    Four fingers o' his right han'.
```

bigget—built
bran' intill—sword into
foreby—aside
gang—go

gar'd—forced . . . to
light leman—whore
mair nor—more than

the morn—on the morrow
thought lang—grew bored
wot—know

The Lowlands of Holland

This would seem to be a typical lament of a sweetheart left behind when her love sails off never to return — but "the lowlands of Holland," just across the Channel, do not seem to be so very far off. Then we realize that her love has sailed off to New Holland — the original name for Australia.

New Hol - land is a bar - ren place, in it there grows no grain, Nor - an - y ha - bi - ta - tion where - in ____ to re - main; But the sug - ar canes are plen - ty and the wine draps frae ___ the ___ tree, And the Low - lands of Hol - land has twin'd my love and me.

E		A		E		A
My love has built a bonny ship, and set her on the sea,

| E | | A | | E | | G♯m |
With seven score good mariners to bear her company;

| E | C♯m | | E7 | | A |
There's threescore is sunk and threescore dead at sea,

| E | | A | | E | B7 | E |
And the Lowlands of Holland has twin'd my love and me.

| E | | A | | E | | A |
My love he built another ship and set her on the main,

| E | | A | | E | | G♯m |
And nane but twenty mariners for to bring her hame;

| E | C♯m | | E7 | | A |
But the weary wind began to rise and the sea began to rout,

| E | | A | | E | B7 | E |
My love then and his bonny ship turn'd withershins about.

| E | | A | | E | | A |
There shall neither coif come on my head nor comb come on my hair,

| E | | A | | E | | G♯m |
There shall neither coal nor candle light shine in my bower mair,

| E | C♯m | | E7 | | A |
Nor will I love another one until the day I die,

| E | | A | | E | B7 | E |
For I never lov'd a love but one and he's drowned in the sea.

| E | | A | | E | | A |
O hold your tongue my daughter dear, be still and be content,

| E | | A | | E | | G♯m |
There are mair lads in Galloway, ye needs nae sair lament;

| E | C♯m | | E7 | | A |
O! there is none is Gallow, there's none at a' for me,

| E | | A | | E | B7 | E |
For I never lov'd a love but one and he's drowned in the sea.

coif—cap   **has twin'd**—have parted   **rout**—roar   **withershins**—the wrong way

Bonnie Dundee

John Graham of Claverhouse, Viscount Dundee (c. 1649–1689), was a dashing Scottish soldier in the service of Charles II. In January 1681 he was appointed to the sherrifships of Wigtown, Dumfries, Kirkcudbright, and Annandale, where he exercised power of life and death over the rebellious population. His motto: "Death, desolation, ruin, and decay." He was killed on July 27, 1689, while leading his victorious Highlanders in the battle of Killiecrankie. The death of Dundee, in the midst of a cavalry charge, formed the subject of numerous legends, the best known of which is that he was invulnerable to all bullets and was killed by a silver button from his own coat. This was the beginning and the end of the first Jacobite revolt.

Borrowing a good tune when they heard one, the supporters of General George B. McClellan, who waged an unsuccessful campaign against Abraham Lincoln in 1864, sang: "...We will rise to his standard three million times three—and the head of our nation McClellan shall be!"

Words by Sir Walter Scott
Music: traditional

Dundee he is mounted, he rides up the street,
The bells they ring backwards, the drums they are beat,
And the Provost (good man) said, "Just e'en let him be,
For the town is well rid of that Bonnie Dundee."   *Chorus*

Then away to the hills, to the lea, to the rocks,
Ere I own a usurper I'll couch with a fox;
So tremble, false whigs, in the midst of your glee,
You have not seen the last of your Bonnie Dundee.   *Chorus*

53

There's Three Brave Loyal Fellows

This song may have been composed on the eve of the battle of Killiecrankie in 1689. The Lindsay mentioned here is probably Colin, Earl of Balcarras, and "the true MacLean" is surely the young Chief of Skye who played such a valliant part at Killiecrankie.

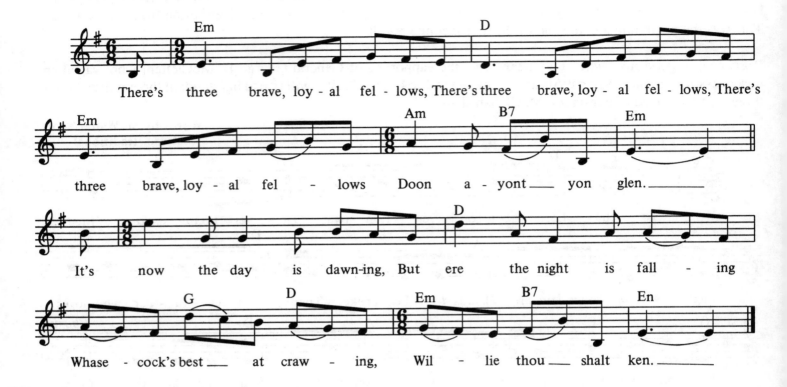

There's three brave, loy-al fel-lows, There's three brave, loy-al fel-lows, There's three brave, loy-al fel - lows Doon a-yont__ yon glen.__ It's now the day is dawn-ing, But ere the night is fall - ing Whase - cock's best __ at craw - ing, Wil - lie thou __ shalt ken. __

Em
There's Graham, Graham and Gordon,
D
Brave Lindsay is coming,
Em
Ken ye wha is running
Am   B7   Em
Wi' his Highlandmen?

'Tis he that's aye the foremost
D
When the battle is warmest,
G   D
The bravest and the kindest
Em B7   Em
Of all Highlandmen.

Em
There's Skye's noble chieftain,
D
Hector and bold Evan,
Em
Reoch, Bane Macrabrach,
Am   B7   Em
And the true MacLean.

Now there's no retreating,
D
For the clans are waiting,
G   D
Every heart is beating,
Em   B7   Em
For honour and for fame.

Repeat first verse

ken—know   **Whase**—Whose

The Haughs o' Cromdale

Scots balladeer Ewen MacColl writes: "Poetic license has been strained to the breaking point in this vigorous ballad. The battle fought upon the plains of Cromdale in Strathspey [May 1, 1690] did, in fact, result in the army of 1,500 Highlanders being defeated by Sir Thomas Livingston's Hanoverians. Montrose, the hero of the song, was not present at the event. Some 45 years before, however, he won a victory at the battle of Auldearn against the Whig forces, and it is probable that the two events have been dovetailed to provide us with a fine, optimistic, if somewhat chronologically inaccurate song." (From the liner notes of *Songs of Two Rebellions,* a 1960 Folkways recording.)

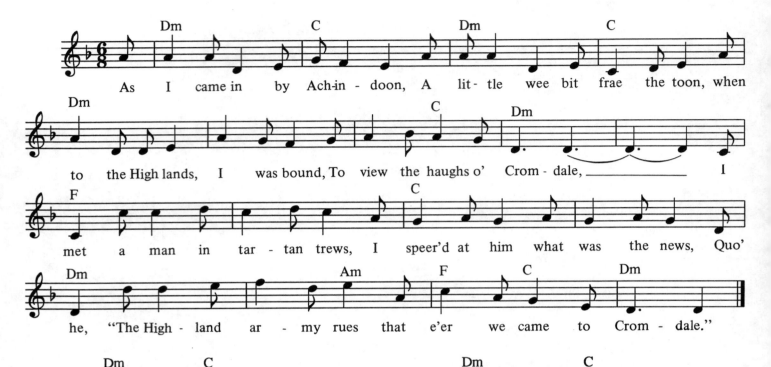

As I came in by Ach-in-doon, A lit-tle wee bit frae the toon, when to the High lands, I was bound, To view the haughs o' Crom-dale, _____ I met a man in tar-tan trews, I speer'd at him what was the news, Quo' he, "The High-land ar-my rues that e'er we came to Crom-dale."

Dm   C
We were in bed, sir, every man,
         Dm   C
When the English host upon us came;
Dm
A bloody battle then began,
            C   Dm
Upon the haughs o' Cromdale.
 F
The English horses they were so rude,
          C
They bathed their hoofs in Highland blood,
  Dm   Am
But our brave clans they boldly stood
  F   C   Dm
Upon the haughs o' Cromdale.

  Dm   C
Alas! we could no longer stay,
  Dm   C
For o'er the hills we came away,
   Dm
And sore we do lament the day
         C   Dm
That e'er we cam to Cromdale.
 F
Thus the great Montrose did say,
   C
"Can you direct the nearest way?
  Dm   Am
For I will o'er the hills this day,
  F   C   Dm
And view the haughs o' Cromdale."

Dm   C
Alas, my lord, you're no' sae strong,
         Dm   C
You scarcely have two thousand men,
         Dm
And there's twenty thousand on the plain,
           C   Dm
Stand rank and file on Cromdale.
 F
Thus the great Montrose did say,
   C
"I say, direct the nearest way,
  Dm   Am
For I will o'er the hills this day,
  F   C   Dm
And see the haughs o' Cromdale."

         Dm   C
They were at dinner, every man,
         Dm   C
When great Montrose upon them came;
         Dm
A second battle then began,
          C   Dm
Upon the haughs o' Cromdale.
         F
The Grant, MacKenzie and McKay,
         C
Soon as Montrose they did espy,
         Dm   Am
O, then they faught most valiantly,
         F   C   Dm
Upon the haughs o' Cromdale.

```
      Dm            C
The MacDonalds they returned again,
      Dm            C
The Camerons did their standard join,
   Dm
MacIntosh played a bloody game
           C        Dm
Upon the haughs o' Cromdale.
           F
The MacGregors fought like lions bold,
      C
The MacPhersons, none could them control,
      Dm                    Am
MacLauchlins fought like loyal souls,
   F      C      Dm
Upon the haughs o' Cromdale.
```

```
      Dm                    C
MacLeans, MacDougals, and MacNeils,
      Dm              C
Sae boldly as they took the field,
      Dm
And made their enemies to yield,
              C        Dm
Upon the haughs o' Cromdale.
           F
The Gordons boldly did advance,
      C
The Frazers faught with sword and lance,
      Dm                      Am
The Grahams they made the heads to dance,
   F      C      Dm
Upon the haughs o' Cromdale.
```

```
         Dm              C
The loyal Stewarts, with Montrose,
      Dm        C
So boldly set upon their foes,
         Dm
And brought them down with Highland blows,
              C        Dm
Upon the haughs o' Cromdale.
           F
Of twenty thousand Cromwell's men,
           C
Five hundred fled to Aberdeen,
      Dm                    Am
The rest of them lie on the plain,
      F      C      Dm
Upon the haughs o' Cromdale.
```

haughs—level ground beside a stream   **toon**—town
speer'd—asked   **trews**—trousers

57

Came Ye O'er Frae France?

King George I was a German from the House of Hanover. When he assumed the English throne in 1714, he imported his seraglio of impoverished German gentlewomen and provided Jacobite songwriters with unparalleled material for some of their most ribald verses. His favorite mistress, Madame Schulemberg, afterwards created Duchess of Kendall, was given the name of "The Goose" in honor of her lean and haggard appearance. She is the "goosie" in this song. The "blade" is Count Königsmark. "Bobbing John" is a reference to John, Earl of Mar, who at the time this song was written was recruiting Highlanders for the Hanoverian cause. "Geordie Whelps" is, of course, none other than George I.

Came ye o'er frae France? Came ye doon by Lun-non?
Saw ye Geor-die Whelps and his bon-nie wo-man? were ye at the place
C'ad the Kit-tle Hous-ie, Saw ye Geor-die's grace rid-ing on a goos-ie?

Dm
Geordie he's the man,
    C
There is little doubt o't;
Dm
He's done a' he can,
F   C
Wha can do without it?
 Dm
Down there came a blade,

Linkin like my lordie;
Am
He would drive a trade
C   Dm
At the loom o' Geordie .

Dm
Though the claith were bad,
      C
Blythely may we niffer;
Dm
Gin we get a wab,
F   C
It makes little differ.
Dm
We hae tint our plaid,

Bonnet, belt and swordie,
Am
Ha's and mailins braid
C   Dm
But we hae a Geordie!

Dm
Jocky's gane to France,
     C
And Montgomery's lady;
Dm
There they'll learn to dance:
F   C
Madam, are you ready?
Dm
They'll be back belyve,

Belted, brisk and lordly:
 Am
Brawly may they thrive
  C   Dm
To dance a jig wi' Geordie!

Dm
Hey for Sandy Don!
      C
Hey for Cockalorum!
Dm
Hey for Bobbing John,
F   C
And his Highland quorum;
Dm
Mony a sword and lance

Swings at Highland hurdie;
Am
How they'll skip and dance
C   Dm
Over the bum o' Geordie;

belyve—quickly
Brawly—Well
claith—cloth
doon—down
gane—gone
Gin—If
Ha's and maillins—Houses and farmlands
hurdie—buttock
Kittle Housie—a house for dancing; alternatively, a house for cats, a brothel
linkin—tripping along
Lunnon—London
niffer—haggle, exchange
tint—lost
wab—web, a length of cloth

The Wee, Wee German Lairdie

George I is mercilessly lampooned in this rollicking song. The terminology employed is that of a Scots gardener.

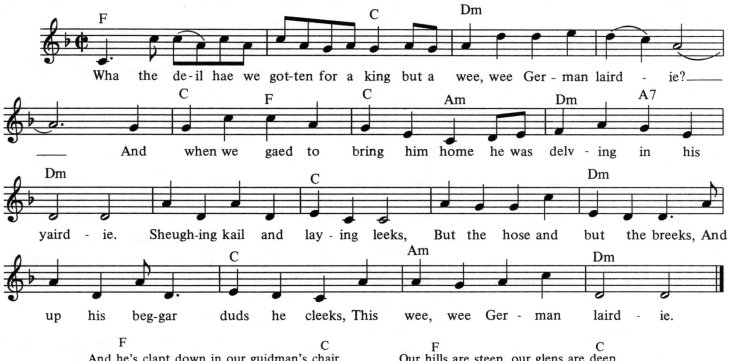

Wha the de-il hae we got-ten for a king but a wee, wee Ger-man laird - ie?____

____ And when we gaed to bring him home he was delv - ing in his

yaird - ie. Sheugh-ing kail and lay - ing leeks, But the hose and but the breeks, And

up his beg-gar duds he cleeks, This wee, wee Ger - man laird - ie.

F   C
And he's clapt down in our guidman's chair,
Dm
This wee, wee German lairdie;
C F C Am
And he's brought fouth o' foreign trash,
Dm A7 Dm
And dibbled them in his yairdie.
      C
He's pu'd the rose o' English loons,
      Dm
And broken the harp o' Irish clowns;
        C
But our thistle taps will jag his thumbs
Am   Dm
This wee, wee German lairdie.

   F   C
Come up amang our Highland hills,
  Dm
Thou wee bit German lairdie,
  C F C Am
And see how the Stuart's lang kail thrive
Dm A7 Dm
They dibbled in our yairdie;
      C
And if a stock ye dare to pu'
     Dm
Or haud the yokin' o' a plough,
       C
We'll break your sceptre ower your mou',
 Am   Dm
Thou wee bit German lairdie.

F   C
Our hills are steep, our glens are deep,
Dm
Nae fitting for a yairdie;
C F C Am
Our Norland thistles winna pu',
  Dm A7 Dm
Thou wee bit German lairdie;
       C
We've the trenching blades o' weir,
       Dm
Wad prune ye o' your German gear,
        C
We'll pass ye 'neath the claymore's shear,
  Am   Dm
Thou feckless German lairdie.

F   C
Auld Scotland, thou'rt ower cauld a hole,
Dm
For nursin' siccan vermin;
    C F C Am
But the very dogs o' England's court,
  Dm A7 Dm
They bark and howl in German.
         C
Then keep thy dibble in thy ain hand,
      Dm
Thy spade but and thy yairdie,
       C
For wha the deil now claims your land,
  Am   Dm
But a wee, wee German lairdie.

But the hose and but the breeks—
 Without hose and trousers
clapt—sat down hastily
claymore's shear—Highland sword
delving—digging
dibbled—planted
fouth—abundance
gaed—went

gear—goods
guidman's chair—throne
haud—hold
lairdie—small landowner
laying leeks—planting vegetables
loons—knaves
mou'—mouth
ower cauld—too cold

pu'd—pulled
siccan—such
taps—tops
weir—war
Wha the deil hae—Who the devil have
winna pu'—will not pull
yairdie—garden

Donald MacGillavry

MacGillavry of Drumglass is one of the chiefs mentioned in the Chevalier's Muster Roll of the 1715 Rebellion. In the rebellion of 1745, the powerful clan M'Intosh was led by a Colonel MacGillavry. A third possibility is that the name might have been used as a general designation for loyal Highlanders.

Don - ald's gane up the hill hard and hun - gry, Don - ald comes down the hill wild and an - gry Don - ald will clear the gouk's nest clev - er - ly, Here's to the king and Don - ald Mac - Gil - lav - ry. Come like a weigh - bauk, Don - ald Mac - Gil - lav - ry, Come like a weigh - bauk, Don - ald Mac - Gil - la - vry, Bal - ance them fair and bal - ance them clev - er - ly. Off wi' the coun - ter - feit, Don - ald Mac-Gil - lav - ry.

Em
Donald's run o'er the hill but his tether, man,
D
As he were wud or stanged wi' an ether, man;
Em
When he comes back, there's some will look merrily:
Am   G   Am   D
Here's to King James and Donald MacGillavry.

Em
Come like a weaver, Donald MacGillavry,
D
Come like a weaver, Donald MacGillavry,
Em
Pack on your back and elwand sae cleverly:
Am   G   Am   D
Gie them full measure, my Donald MacGillavry.

Em
Donald has foughten wi' rief and roguery;
D
Donald has dinner'd wi' banes and beggary;
Em
Better it were for Whigs and Whiggery,
Am   G   Am   D
Meeting the devil than Donald MacGillavry.

Em
Come like a tailor, Donald MacGillavry,
D
Come like a tailor, Donald MacGillavry,
Em
Push them about, in and out, themble them cleverly;
Am   G   Am   D
Here's to King James and Donald MacGillavry;

Em
Donald's the callan that brooks nae tangleness;
D
Whigging and prigging and a' newfangleness,
Em
They maun be gane: he winna be baukit, man:
Am   G   Am   D
He maun hae justice, or faith, he'll tak it, man,

Em
Come like a cobbler, Donald MacGillavry,
D
Come like a cobbler, Donald MacGillavry;
Em
Beat them and bore them and lingel them cleverly.
Am   G   Am   D
Up wi' King James and Donald MacGillavry.

Em
Donald was mumpit wi' mirds and mockery;
D
Donald was blinded wi' blads o' property;
Em
Arles ran high but makings were naething,
Am   G   Am   D
Lord, how Donald is flyting and fretting,

Em
Come like the devil, Donald MacGillavry,
D
Come like the devil, Donald MacGillavry;
Em
Skelp them and scaud them that proved sae unbritherly.
Am   G   Am   D
"Up wi' King James and Donald MacGillavry.

Arles—Thrashing
banes—bones
baukit—balked
blads—large portions
but—without
callan—fine fellow

elwand—measuring rod
flyting—scolding
gouk's nest—cuckoo's nest
lingel—shoemaker's thread
mumpit wi' mirds—lulled with flattery
rief—banditry

scaud—scold
Skelp—Chastise
stanged wi' an ether—stung by an adder
weigh-bauk—scales
wud—mad

The Piper O' Dundee

Sir Walter Scott suggests that the unknown piper may be the notable Carnegie of Phinhaven. All those mentioned in the song were leading Jacobites.

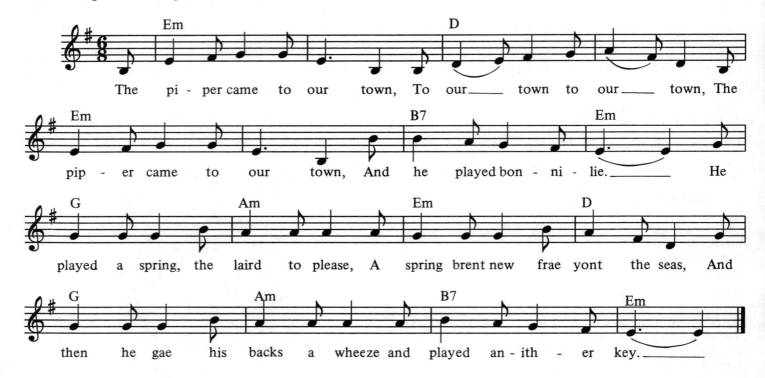

The pi-per came to our town, To our___ town to our___ town, The pip-er came to our town, And he played bon-ni-lie.___ He played a spring, the laird to please, A spring brent new frae yont the seas, And then he gae his backs a wheeze and played an-ith-er key.___

Chorus - sung to first 8 measures

Em
And wasna he a roguey,

D
A roguey, a roguey?

Em
And wasna he a roguey,

B7   Em
The piper o' Dundee?

Verses - sung to last 8 measures

G   Am
He play'd "The Welcome Ower the Main,"

Em   D
And "Ye's Be Fou and I'se Be Fain,"

G   Am
And "Auld Stuart's Back Again'"

B7   Em
Wi' muckle mirth and glee. *Chorus*

G   Am
He play'd "The Kirk," he play'd "The Queer,"

Em   D
"The Mullin Dhu," and "Chevalier,"

G   Am
And "Lang Awa' But Welcome Here,"

B7   Em
Sae sweet, sae bonnilie. *Chorus*

G   Am
It's some gat swords and some gat nane,

Em   D
And some were dancing mad their lane,

G   Am
And mony a vow o' weir was ta'en

B7   Em
That night at Amulrie. *Chorus*

G   Am
There was Tullibardine and Burleigh,

Em   D
And Struan, Keith and Ogilvie,

G   Am
And brave Carnegie, wha but he,

B7   Em
The piper o' Dundee. *Chorus*

brent new—brand new
gat—have
laird—landowner
mad their lane—on their own

muckle mirth—great mirth
nane—none
Queer—Choir
spring—dance

weir—war
"Ye's Be Fou and I'se Be Fain"—
   "You're full, I'm willing"
'yont—beyond

Will Ye Go to Sheriffmuir?

The battle of Sheriffmuir was fought on November 13, 1715, between the clans under the Earl of Mar and the Hanoverian forces (supporters of the British crown) under the Duke of Argyle. Though the Jacobites were clearly the winners in the song department, the actual military victory was claimed by both sides.

There's some that say that we wan,
And some that say that they wan,
And some say that nane wan at a' man;
But, one thing, I'm sure
That at Sheriffmuir,
A battle there was which I saw, man.
And we ran, and they ran,
And they ran, and we ran,
And we ran, and they ran awa' man.

Will ye go to Sher-if-muir, Bauld John o' In-nis-ture, There to see the no-ble Mar And his High-land lad-dies. A' the true men o' the North, An-gus, Hunt-ley and Sea-forth, Scour-ing on to cross the Forth, Wi' their white cock-a-dies?

D
There ye'll see the banners flare,
A7
There ye'll hear the bagpipes rair,
D
And the trumpets' deadly blare,
A7 D
Wi' the cannon's rattle.

There ye'll see the bauld McCraws,
Em   A7
Camerons and Clanronald's raws,
D
And a' the clans wi' loud huzzas,
A7 D
Rushing to the battle.

D
There ye'll see the noble whigs,
A7
A the heroes o' the brigs,
D
Raw hides and withered wigs,
A7   D
Riding in array, man.

Ri'en hose and raggit hools,
Em   A7
Sour milk and girnin gools,
D
Psalm-beuks and cutty-stools,
A7   D
We'll see never mair man.

D
Will ye go to Sheriffmuir,
A7
Bauld John o' Innisture?
D
Sic a day and sic an hour,
A7   D
Ne'er was in the North, man.

Siccan sights there will be seen;
Em   A7
And, gin some be nae mista' en,
D
Fragrant gales will come bedeen,
A7   D
Frae the water o' Forth, man.

Bauld—Bold
cutty stools—stools on which unmarried
  mothers had to sit in church when they
  made their confessions
gin—if

girnin gools—weeping melancholics
hools—clothing
mista'en—mistaken
Psalm-beuks—Psalm books

raws—rows
Ri'en—Torn
sic—such
Siccan—Such

Johnny Cope

English General John Cope was defeated by the Jacobite army under the command of Prince Charlie at the battle of Prestonpans on September 21, 1745.

Cope sent a chal-lenge frae Dun-bar, "Char-lie meet me, an' ye daur, And I'll learn ye the art of war, If you meet me in ___ the morn - in'."

Chorus

Hey, John-nie cope, are ye wauk-in yet? or are your drums a-beat-in yet? If ye were wauk-in I would wait to gang to the coals ___ in the morn - ing.

Dm / C
When Charlie looked this letter upon,

He drew his sword the scabbard from,
Dm C Dm
"Come follow me, my merry men,
A7 Dm
An' we'll meet Johnnie Cope in the morning." *Chorus*

Dm / C
"Now, Johnnie, be as good as your word,

And try your faith with fire and sword,
Dm C Dm
And dinna flee awa' like a frightened bird
A7 Dm
That's chased frae its nest in the morning." *Chorus*

Dm / C
When Johnnie Cope he heard o' this,

He thocht it wouldna be amiss
Dm C Dm
To hae a horse in readiness,
A7 Dm
For to flee awa' in the morning. *Chorus*

Dm / C
"C' wa now, Johnnie, get up and rin,

The Hieland bagpipes mak a din.
Dm C Dm
It's best to sleep in a hale skin,
A7 Dm
It will be a bloodie morning." *Chorus*

Dm / C
When Johnnie Cope to Dunbar came,

They speired at him, "Where's a your men?"
Dm C Dm
"The deil confound me gin I ken,
A7 Dm
For I left them a' this morning." *Chorus*

Dm / C
"Noo, Johnnie, troth, ye were na blate,

To leave your men in sic a strait,
Dm C Dm
And come wi' the news o' your ain defeat
A7 Dm
Sae early in the morning." *Chorus*

Dm / C
"In faith," quo' Johnnie, "I got sic flegs,

Wi' their claymores and filabegs,
Dm C Dm
If I face them again, deil break my legs,
A7 Dm
So I wish you a' good morning. *Chorus*

blate—bashful
claymores and filabegs—
  Highland swords and kilts
C'wa—Come away
daur—dare

deil—devil
dinna—do not
flegs—blows
gang—go
gin—if

hae—have
hale—whole
ken—know
rin—run
sic—such

speired—asked
thoucht—thought
waukin—waking

Skye Boat Song

The Duke of Cumberland defeated Charles Edward Stuart — Bonnie Prince Charlie — at the battle of Culloden Moor on April 16, 1746. That effectively put an end to The Young Pretender's hopes to secure the British throne. He was forced to flee to the island of Skye in the inner Hebrides. From there he made his way to France, never to return to Scotland.

Words by Sir Harold Boulton (1884)

Music by Annie McLeod

"Speed bon-nie boat, like a bird on the wing, Onward," the sail - ors cry.____

"Car - ry the lad that's born to be king, O - ver the sea to Skye!"____

Lord the winds howl, loud the waves roar, Thun - der clouds rend the air.____

Baf - fled, our foes stand on the shore, Fol - low they will not dare.____

Em   Am
Though the waves leap, soft shall ye sleep,
Em C Em
Ocean's a royal bed.
     Am
Rock'd in the deep, Flora will keep
Em   C Em D7
Watch by your weary head. *Chorus*

Em   Am
Many's the lad fought on that day,
Em C Em
Well the claymore could wield,
     Am
When the night came, silently lay
Em   C Em D7
Dead on Culloden's field. *Chorus*

Em   Am
Burn'd are our homes, exile and death.
Em C Em
Scatter the loyal men;
     Am
Yet, e'er the sword cool in the sheath,
Em   C Em D7
Charlie will come again. *Chorus*

claymore—a two-handed Highland sword

Bonnie Charlie's Now Awa'

Prince Charles was warmly welcomed to France by Louis XV. He continued his political intrigues in Paris and, although he became a popular hero and idol of the Parisians, he received little political assistance. A condition of the treaty of Aix-la-Chapelle (1748) between England and France was that every member of the house of Stuart be expelled from the French dominions. Charles wandered throughout Europe for years, hoping once again to raise support for the Jacobite cause. Rumor had him in London in 1750 and 1754, hatching futile plots and risking his safety for a hopeless cause. Nothing ever came of his efforts. He died in Rome in 1788.

Words by Lady Mairne
Melody: traditional

E   A   E
Hills he trod were all his ain,
       F♯7   B7
Bed beneath the birken tree.
E   A   E
The bush that hid him on the plain,
     B7   E
None on earth can claim but he. *Chorus*

E   A   E
Sweet the lav'rock's note and lang,
       F♯7   B7
Liltin' wildy up the glen,
E   A   E
But aye to me he sings ae song,
       B7   E
"Will ye no come back again?" *Chorus*

E   A   E
Mony a gallant sodger fought,
       F♯7   B7
Mony a gallant chief did fa'.
E   A   E
Death itself were dearly bought,
       B7   E
A' for Scotland's king and law. *Chorus*

lav(e)rock—lark

Wae's Me for Prince Charlie

Scots ballad makers continued to extol the virtues of Prince Charles for almost another hundred years after the collapse of the rebellion. This lament was written by William Glen, who was born in Glasgow in 1789, the year of another notable revolution.

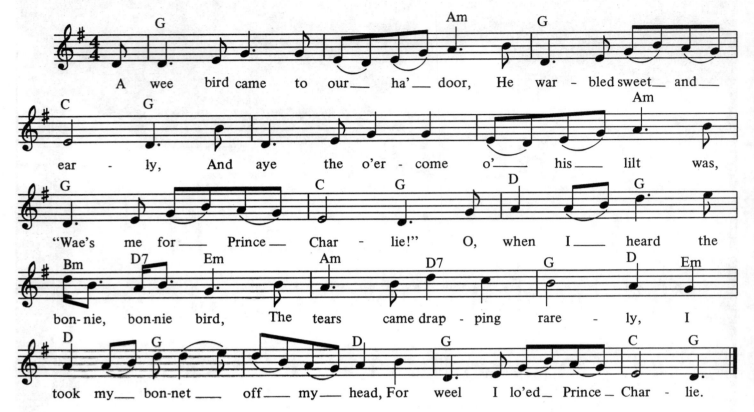

A wee bird came to our ha' door, He warbled sweet and early, And aye the o'ercome o' his lilt was, "Wae's me for Prince Charlie!" O, when I heard the bonnie, bonnie bird, The tears came drapping rarely, I took my bonnet off my head, For weel I lo'ed Prince Charlie.

	G				Am
Said I, "My bird, my bonnie, bonnie bird,

G   C G
Is that a tale ye borrow?

                              Am
Or is't some words ye've learnt by rote,

G   C G
Or a lilt o' dule and sorrow?"

D   G   Bm D7 Em
"O, no, no, no!" the wee bird sang,

Am   D7   G D
"I've flown sin' morning early;

Em D G   D
But sic a day o' wind and rain!

G   C G
O, wae's me for Prince Charlie!"

G   Am
On hills that are by right his ain,

G   C G
He roams a lonely stranger;

                              Am
On ilka hand he's pressed by want,

G   C G
On ilka side by danger.

D   G   Bm D7 Em
Yestreen I met him in a glen,

Am   D7   G D
My hairt near bursted fairly,

Em D G   D
For sadly changed indeed was he,

G   C G
O, wae's me for Prince Charlie!

G   Am
Dark night came on, the tempest howled

G   C G
Out ower the hills and valleys;

                              Am
And where was't that your prince lay down,

G   C G
Whase hame should been a palace?

D   G   Bm D7 Em
He row'd him in a Highland plaid,

Am D7   G D
Which covered him but sparely,

Em D G   D
And slept beneath a bush of broom.

G   C G
O, wae's me for Prince Charlie!

dule—sadness
ha'—hall
hairt—heart

ilka—every
row'd—wrapped
sic—such

Wae's me—Woe is me
weel I lo'ed—well I loved
Yestreen—Yesterday evening

My Bonnie Moorhen

Like protest songs in other times and other places, the Jacobite songs were proscribed. A coded language was often employed to get the message across. Prince Charles Stuart appears in songs often disguised as a blackbird, as "our guidman," and, in this song, as a moorhen. The colors mentioned in the second verse are those found in the Clan Stuart tartan.

My bon-nie moor-hen, my bon-nie moor-hen, Up in the grey hill,____ doon in the glen, It's when ye gang but the house, when ye gang ben,____ Aye__ drink__ a health to my bon-nie moor-hen,_____ My__ bon-nie moor-hen's__ gane o-ver the main, And it will be sim-mer or she comes a-gain, But when she comes back a-gain some folk will ken,____ Joy____ be wi' thee, my bon-nie moor-hen.

My bonnie moorhen has feathers enew,
She's a' fine colours, but nane o' them blue;
She's red and she's white and she's green and she's grey,
My bonnie moorhen, come hither away.
Come up by Glenduich and down by Glendee,
And round by Kinclaven and hither to me;
For Ronald and Donald are out on the fen,
To break the wing o' my bonnie moorhen.

ben—inside   **but**—outside   **simmer**—summer

This Is No My Ain House

Another use of the coded allegory handled so skillfully by Jacobite songwriters. The "house" is, of course, Scotland; "my daddy" is the exiled Stuart king; the "cringing foreign goose" is the Hanoverian usurper.

Very freely
Chorus

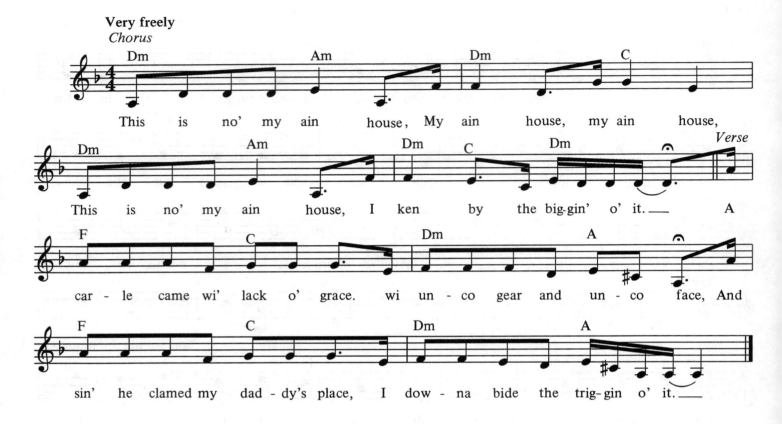

This is no' my ain house, My ain house, my ain house,
This is no' my ain house, I ken by the big-gin' o' it. — A
car - le came wi' lack o' grace. wi un - co gear and un - co face, And
sin' he clamed my dad-dy's place, I dow - na bide the trig-gin o' it. —

F   C
Wi' routh o' kin and routh o' reek,
Dm   A
My daddy's door it wouldna steek;
F   C
But bread and cheese were his door-cheek,
Dm   A
And girdle-cakes the riggin' o't. *Chorus*

F   C
Then was it dink, or was it douce,
Dm   A
For ony cringing foreign goose,
F   C
To claucht daddy's wee bit house,
Dm   A
And spoil the hamely triggin o' t? *Chorus*

F   C
My daddy bag his housie weel,
Dm   A
By dint o' head and dint o' heel,
F   C
By dint o' arm and dint o' steel,
Dm   A
And muckle weary priggin o't. *Chorus*

F   C
Say was it foul or was it fair
Dm   A
To come a hunder mile and mair,
F   C
For to ding out my daddy's heir,
Dm   A
And dash him wi' the whiggin o' t? *Chorus*

ain—own
bag—built
biggin—building
carle—worthless fellow
claucht—seize
dink, or **douce**—seemly, or of good behavior

door-cheek—door step
downa—cannot
ken—know
triggin—decoration
unca—ill-formed
Wi' routh o' kin and routh o' reek—
    With such a large family and so much bustle

Ye Jacobites by Name

"Now there's ane end of ane auld sang." (James Ogilvy, lst earl of Seafield, addressing Parliament in Edinborough on the end of Scottish separate independence, April 28, 1707.)

By Robert Burns

Ye Ja - cob-ites by name,— give an ear, give an ear, Ye
Ja - cob-ites by name,— give an ear. Ye Ja - cob-ites by name, Your
faults I will pro - claim, Your doc - trines I maun blame, You shall
hear, you shall hear, Your doc - trines I maun blame, you shall hear.

Em Bm	Em Bm

         Em   Bm   Em   Bm

Em
What is right and what is wrang, by the law, by the law?
Em   Bm Em
What is right and what is wrang, by the law?
      G
What is right and what is wrang?
  Am
A short sword and a lang,
  Em
A weak arm and a strang
Bm Em   Bm
For to draw, for to draw,
  Em   Bm   Em
A weak arm a strang for to draw.

Em
What makes heroic strife, famed afar, famed afar?
Em   Bm Em
What makes heroic strife famed afar?
      G
What makes heroic strife?
  Am
To whet the assassin's knife,
  Em
Or hunt a parent's life
          Bm Em   Bm
Wi' bloody war, bloody war,
        Em   Bm   Em
Or hunt a parent's life wi' bloody war.

           Em   Bm
Then let your schemes alone, in the state, in the state,
           Em   Bm Em
Then let your schemes alone, in the state.

          G
Then let your schemes alone,
        Am
Adore the rising sun,
          Em
And leave a man undone
Bm Em   Bm
To his fate, to his fate,
         Em   Bm Em
And leave a man undone to his fate.

maun—must

72

Such a Parcel of Rogues

This song embodies pretty fairly the anti-union feeling of Scotland during the 18th century. The charge of corruption which is made against the majority of the Scottish Parliament for "selling out for English gold" is repeated again and again in the Jacobite songs.

by Robert Burns

Em | G
Fare - weel to a' our Scot - tish fame, Fare

Am | C G Em
weel our an - cient glo - ry, Fare - weel e - ven to the

G | Am | C G
Scot - tish name, Sae famed in mar - tial sto - ry, Now

Em | G | Em D
Sark runs o'er the Sol way sands, And Tweed runs to the

Em | G | C
O - cean, To mark where Eng - land's pro - vince stands;

G | Am Bm C | G
Such a par - cel of rogues in a na - tion

Em   G
What force or guile could not subdue,
Am   C G
Through many warlike ages,
Em   G
Is wraught now by a coward few,
Am   C G
For hireling traitor's wages.
Em   G
The English steel we could disdain,
Em   D   Em
Secure in valour's station,
G   C
But English gold has been our bane;
G   Am Bm C G
Such a parcel of rogues in a nation.

Em   G
O would, or I had seen the day
Am   C G
That treason thus could sell us,
Em   G
My auld gray head had lain in clay,
Am   C G
Wi' Bruce and loyal Wallace!
Em   G
But pith and power, till my last hour,
Em   D Em
I'll make this declaration:
G   C
We're bought and sold for English gold;
G   Am Bm C G
Such a parcel of rogues in a nation.

Charlie Is My Darling

This song about Prince Charlie resurfaced during the American Civil War as "Charlie is my darling...the Union volunteer."

Charlie's (the Prince's) extra-military exploits suggested in this song are, as far as we know, totally unfounded. It was not until his exile in France and his subsequent wanderings in Europe that he began to "please the lasses."

By Robert Burns

Chorus

Char - lie is my dar - ling, my dar - ling my dar - ling,
Char - lie is my dar - ling, The young____ chev - a - lier._____ *Fine*

Verse

As he was walk - ing up the street, the cit - y for to view,_____ O,
there he spied a bon - nie lass, The win - dow look - ing through.____

E7 Am Sae light's he jumped up the stair, E7 Am And tirled at the pin; F C And wha sae ready as hersel Dm Am E7 To let the laddie in. *Chorus*	
E7 Am He set his Jenny on his knee, E7 Am All in his Highland dress; F C For brawly weel he kend the way Dm Am E7 To please a bonnie lass. *Chorus*	
E7 Am It's up yon heathery mountain, E7 Am And down yon scraggy glen, F C We daurna gang a-milking Dm Am E7 For Charlie and his men. *Chorus*	

brawly weel he kend—very well he knew   **daurna gang**—dare not go   **wha sae**—who so

Once More I Hail Thee

Beethoven set twelve Irish and Scottish songs for violin, cello and piano.

Music by Ludwig van Beethoven   **Words attributed to Robert Burns**

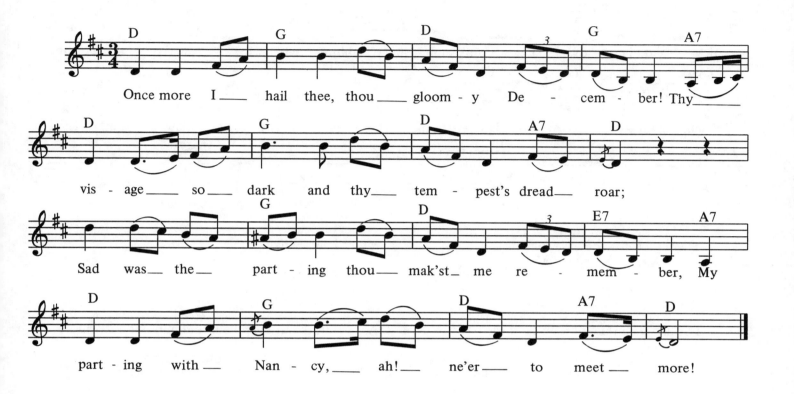

Once more I hail thee, thou gloom-y De-cem-ber! Thy

vis-age so dark and thy tem-pest's dread roar;

Sad was the part-ing thou mak'st me re-mem-ber, My

part-ing with Nan-cy, ah! ne'er to meet more!

    D   G   D   G
Fond lovers parting is sweet painful pleasure,
  A7 D   G   D   A7 D
When hope mildly beams on the soft parting hour;
               G   D   E7
But the dire feeling, "O farewell forever,"
 A7 D   G   D A7 D
Is anguish unmingled and agony pure.

    D   G   D   G
Wild as the winter now tearing the forest,
 A7 D   G   D   A7 D
Until the last leaf of the summer is flown;
               G   D   E7
Such is the tempest has shaken my bosom,
 A7   D   G   D   A7 D
Since hope is departed and comfort is gone.

    D   G   D   G
Still as I hail thee, thou gloomy December,
 A7 D   G   D   A7 D
My anguish awakes at thy visage so hoar;
               G   D   E7
Sad was the parting thou mak'st me remember,
 A7 D   G   D   A7 D
My parting with Nancy, ah, ne'er to meet more!

Guidwife, Count the Lawin'

By Robert Burns

Gone is the day, and mirk's the night, but we'll ne'er stray for want o' light, For ale and bran-dy's stars and moon, and blood-red wine's the ris-ing sun.

Chorus

Then, guid wife count the law - in, The law - in, the law - in, Then guid wife count the law - in, And bring a cog-gie mair.

C   Am   G   Em
There's wealth and ease for gentlemen,
Am   C
And semple folk maun fecht and fen' ;
D7   G   Em
But here we're a' in ae accord,
Am   C
For ilka man that's drunk's a lord. *Chorus*

C   Am   G   Em
My coggie is a haly pool,
Am   C
That heals the wounds o' care and dool,
D7   G   Em
And pleasure is a wanton trout,
Am   C
An' ye drink but deep ye'll find him out. *Chorus*

coggie—jug
dool—trouble

ilka—every
lawin—reckoning or bill

maun fecht and fen'—
must fight and struggle

Hey, the Dusty Miller

By Robert Burns

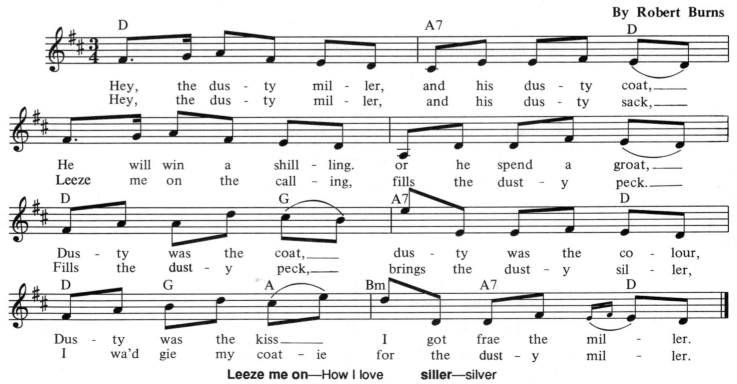

Hey,   the dus-ty mil-ler,   and his dus-ty coat,____
Hey,   the dus-ty mil-ler,   and his dus-ty sack,____

He   will win a shill-ling.   or he spend a groat,____
Leeze me on the call-ing, fills the dust-y peck.____

Dus-ty was the coat,____   dus-ty was the co-lour,
Fills the dust-y peck,____   brings the dust-y sil-ler,

Dus-ty was the kiss____   I got frae the mil-ler.
I   wa'd gie my coat-ie for the dust-y mil-ler.

Leeze me on—How I love   **siller**—silver

76

My Luve Is Like a Red, Red Rose

By Robert Burns

O, my love is like a red, red rose that's new - ly sprung in June; O, my luve is like a mel - o - die that's swee - tly played in tune! As fair art thou, my bon - nie lass, so deep in love am I____ And____ I will luve thee still my dear, till a' the seas gang dry. Till a' the seas gang dry, my dear, till a' the seas gang dry; And____ I will love thee still, my dear, Till a' the seas gang dry.

<pre>
                A   F#m
'Til a' the seas gang dry, my dear,
        D   E7
And the rocks melt wi' the sun,
        A   F#m
An I will luve thee still, my dear,
        D   E7   A
While the sands of life shall run.
                      D   A
But, fare thee weel, my only luve!
        E7
O fare thee weel awhile!
      A   D   A
And I will come again, my luve,
      E7   A
Tho' 'twere ten thousand mile.
                           F#m
Tho' 'twere ten thousand mile, my luve,
            D   E7
Tho' 'twere ten thousand mile,
      A   F#m
And I will come again, my luve,
        D   E7   A
Tho' 'twere ten thousand mile.
</pre>

77

Is There for Honest Poverty
(A Man's a Man for a' That)

Robert Burns: "A great critic (Aikin) on songs says that Love and Wine are the exclusive themes for song-writing. The following is on neither subject and consequently is no song.... I do not give you the foregoing song for your book, but merely by way of *vive la bagatelle;* for the piece is not really poetry." Whether Burns was serious or not in this 1795 letter we cannot say, but one thing is certain—this song has come to represent some of the most exalted sentiments felt by humanity.

By Robert Burns

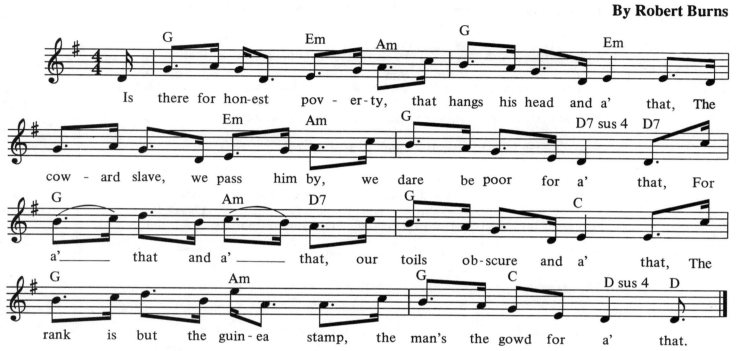

<pre>
          G   Em   Am   G   Em
What tho' on homely fare we dine, wear hodden gray and a' that,
          G   Em   Am   G   D7sus4 D7
Gie fools their silk and knaves their wine, a man's a man for a'   that.
          G   Am D7   G   C
For a' that and a' that, their tinsel show and a' that,
          G   Am   G   C   Dsus4   D
The honest man, tho' e'er sae poor is king o' men for a'   that.

          G   Em   Am   G   Em
Ye see yon birkie called a lord, who struts and stares and a' that,
          G   Em   Am   G   D7sus4 D7
Tho' hundreds worship at his word, he's but a cuif for a'   that.
          G   Am D7   G   C
For a' that and a' that, his ribband star and a' that,
          G   Am   G   C   D sus 4 D
The man of independent mind, he looks and laughs at a'   that.

          G   Em   Am   G   Em
A prince can make a belted knight, a marquis, duke and a' that,
          G   Em   Am   G   D7sus4 D7
But an honest man's above his might, **good** faith he keeps for a'   that.
          G   Am D7   G   C
For a' that and a' that, their dignities and a' that,
          G   Am   G   C   Dsus4   D
The pith o' sense and pride o' worth are higher rank than a'   that.

          G   Em   Am   G   Em
Then let us pray that come it may, as come it will for a' that,
          G   Em   Am   G   D7sus4 D7
That sense and worth o'er a' the earth shall win the fight for a'   that.
          G   Am D7   G   C
For a' that and a' that, it's comin' yet for a' that,
          G   Am   G   C   D sus 4 D
That man to man the world o'er shall brothers be for a'   that.
</pre>

birkie—fellow
cuif—fool
gowd—fool
hodden gray—coarse gray woolen

The Bonniest Lass

(Tune: Is There for Honest Poverty)

```
         G          Em    Am     G          Em
The bonniest lass that ye meet neist, gie her a kiss an' a' that,
    G          Em    Am     G          D7sus4 D7
In spite o' ilka parish priest, repentin' stool, an' a'  that,
    G       Am       G              C
For a' that an' a' that, their mim—mou'd sangs an' a that,
    G          Am        G         Dsus4 D
In time and place convenient, they'll do't themselves, for a   that.


        G         Em    Am     G           Em
Your patriarchs in days o' yore had their handmaids an' a' that,
    G          Em    Am    G             D7sus4 D7
O' bastard gets, some had a score - and some had mair than  a'  that.
    G      Am D7    G           C
For a' that an' a' that, your langsyne saunts an' a' that
    G       Am         G         Dsus4 D7
Were fonder o' a bonnie lass than you or I, for  a'   that.


       G         Em    Am      G           Em
King Davie, when he waxed auld, an's bluid ran thin an' a' that,
    G         Em    Am      G             D7sus4 D7
An' fand his cods were growin' cauld, could not refrain for  a'  that.
    G       Am       G          C
For a' that an' a' that, to keep him warm an' a' that,
    G          Am        G         Dsus4 D
The daughters o' Jerusalem were waled for him, an' a' that.


       G         Em       Am     G           Em
Wha wadna pity thae sweet dames he fumbled at, an' a' that,
    G          Em    Am    G             D7sus4 D7
An' raised their bluid up into flames he couldna drown for  a'   that.
    G      Am D7    G           C
For a' that an' a' that, he wanted pith an' a' that,
    G          Am              G            Dsus4 D
For, as to what, we shall not name - what could he do but claw that.


       G         Em    Am     G            Em
King Solomon, prince o' divines, wha proverbs made, an' a' that,
    G          Em    Am    G          D7sus4 D
Baith mistresses an' concubines in hundreds had, for  a'  that.
    G       Am         G          C
For a' that an' a' that, tho' preacher wise, an a' that,
    G          Am            G             D7sus4 D
The smuttiest sang that e'er was sung - his Sang O' Sangs is   a'  that.


      G          Em    Am     G            Em
Then still I swear, a clever chiel should kiss a lass, an' a' that,
       G          Em    Am   G            D7sus4 D7
Tho' priests consign him to the deil, as reprobate an'   a'   that.
    G       Am D7    G            C
For a' that an' a' that, their canting stuff an' a' that,
    G              Qm         G         Dsus4 D
They ken nae mair wha's reprobate than you or I, for  a'  that.
```

bluid—blood	**ken nae**—know no	**neist**—next
chiel—young fellow	**langsyne saunts**—old-time saints	**pith**—strength
deil—devil	**mair**—more	**waled**—picked
ilka—every	**mim-mou'd**—mealy-mouthed	

Auld Lang Syne

Robert Burns: " 'Auld Lang Syne'—the air is but mediocre; but the following song—the old song of the olden times, and which has never been in print, nor even in manuscript, until I took it down from an old man's singing, is enough to recommend any air."

By Robert Burns

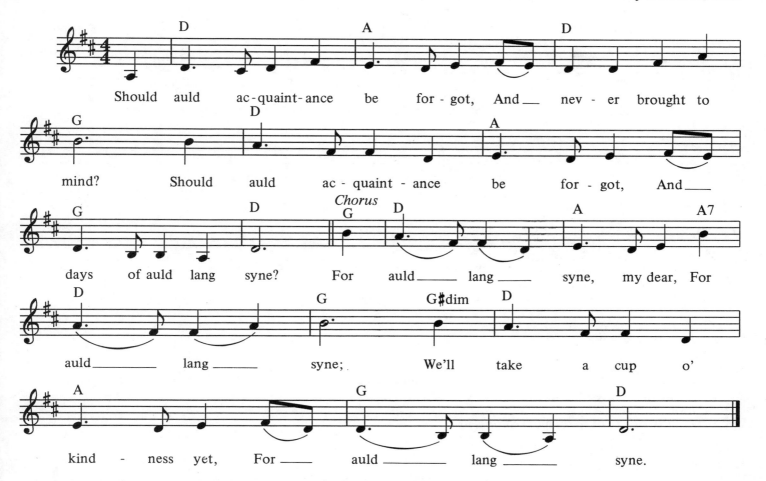

We twa ha'e ran aboot the braes
And pu'd the gowans fine,
We've wandered many a weary foot,
Sin auld lang syne. *Chorus*

We twa ha'e sported i'the burn
Frae mornin' sun till dine,
But seas between us braid ha'e roared,
Sin auld lang syne. *Chorus*

And here's a hand my trusty frien',
And gie's a hand o' thine;
We'll tak' a cup o' kindness yet,
For auld lang syne. *Chorus*

auld lang syne—old bygone days
braes—hillocks

burn—a rivulet
gowans—wild daisies

Green Grow the Rashes, O

By Robert Burns

There's_ naught but care on ev-'ry han' In ev-'ry hour that pass-es o; What sig-ni-fies that life o' man, An' 'twere not for the las-ses o?

Chorus

Green_ grow the rash-es o. Green_ grow the rash-es o; The sweet-est hours that-e'er I spend, Are spent a-mong_ the las-ses, o.

        C   Am
The war'ly race may riches chase,
        Dm   F   Dm
An' riches still may fly them, O;
        F   C
An' tho' at last they catch them fast,
        Dm   E7   Am
Their hearts can ne'er enjoy them, O. *Chorus*

        C   Am
But gie me a cannie hour at e'en,
        Dm   F   Dm
My arms about my dearie, O,
        F   C
An' war'ly cares an' war'ly men
        Dm   E7 Am
May a' gae tapsalteerie, O! *Chorus*

        C   Am
For you sae douce, ye sneer at this;
        Dm   F   Dm
Ye're nought but senseless asses, O;
        F   C
The wisest man the warl' e'er saw,
        Dm   E7   Am
He dearly lov'd the lasses, O. *Chorus*

        C   Am
Auld Nature swears, the lovely dears
        Dm   F   Dm
Her noblest work she classes, O:
        F   C
Her prentice han' she try'd on man,
        Dm   E7   Am
An' then she made the lasses, O. *Chorus*

cannie—quiet **douce**—serious **tapsalteerie**—topsy turvey

82

John Highlandman

By Robert Burns

With his philibeg, an' tartan plaid,
    C
An' guid claymore down by his side,
       G
The ladies' hearts he did trepan,
C   **G Am**
My gallant, braw John Highlandman. *Chorus*
F **G7**   **C**

We ranged a' from Tweed to Spey,
   C
An' liv'd like lords an' ladies gay,
       G
For a Lalland face he feared none,
   C   **G Am**
My gallant, braw John Highlandman. *Chorus*
F **G7**   **C**

They banish'd him beyond the sea,
     C
But ere the bud was on the tree,
        G
Adown my cheeks the pearls ran,
C   **C Am**
Embracing my John Highlandman. *Chorus*
F **G7**   **C**

But Och! they catch'd him at the last,
     C
And bound him in a dungeon fast.
        G
My curse upon them every one
  C   **G Am**
They've hang'd my braw John Highlandman! *Chorus*
F **G7**   **C**

And now a widow I must mourn
    C
The pleasures that will ne'er return;
       G
No comfort but a hearty can,
   C   **G Am**
When I think on John Highlandman. *Chorus*
F **G7**   **C**

braw—handsome   **claymore**—a two-handed Highland sword   **Lalland**—lowland   **philibeg**—Highlander's kilt

O, Whistle an' I'll Come to Ye, Me Lad

By Robert Burns

Chorus

O,— whis-tle an' I'll— come to ye, my lad! O, whis-tle an' I'll— come to ye, my lad! Tho' fa-ther and moth-er and a' should gae mad, O,— whis-tle an' I'll— come to ye, my lad!

Verse

But war-i-ly tent when ye come to court me, And come nae un-less the back yett be a-jee; Syne up the back style, and let nae-bod-y see, And— come as ye were-na com-in to me!

| G | | |
| At kirk, or at market, whene'er ye meet me, | | |

                         A7   D7
Gang by me as tho' that ye car'd na a flie;
    G   Bm
But steal me a blink o' your bonie black e'e,
    G   Em   G
Yet look as ye were na lookin to me! *Chorus*

    G
Ay vow and protest that ye care na for me,
                            A7   D7
And whyles ye may lightly my beauty a wee,
    G   Em
But court na anither tho' jokin ye be,
    G   Em   G
For fear that she wyle your fancy frae me. *Chorus*

back yett be ajee—back gate be open

Flow Gently, Sweet Afton

Robert Burns:" . . . (intended as a) compliment (to the) small river Afton that flows into Nith, near New Cummock, which has some charming wild romantic scenery on its banks."

Music by Alexander Hume
Words by Robert Burns

Flow gent - ly, sweet_ Af - ton, a - mong thy green braes; Flow gent - ly, I'll

sing thee a song in thy praise; My Mar - y's a___ sleep by thy

mur - mur - ing stream, Flow gent - ly, sweet Af - ton, dis - turb not her

dream. Thou_ stock dove, whose ech - o re - sounds from the hill, Ye___

mild whis - tling black - birds in yon'___ thorn - y___ dell, Thou

green crest - ed ___ lap - wing, thy scream - ing for - bear. I

charge you, dis - turb not my slum - ber ing fair.

```
      D        A7   D        G
How lofty sweet Afton, thy neighboring hills
  A7  D     A7        D                E7  A
Far marked with the courses of clear winding rills.
  A7    D A7 D       G        D
There daily I wander as morn rises high,
  A7   D       A   D D7 G  A7        D
My flocks and my Mary's sweet cot in my eye.
      A                        E7        A
How pleasant thy banks and green valleys below,
                        E7      A
Where wild in the woodlands the primroses blow.
  A7   D   F#7  Bm    D    G       D
There oft as mild evening creeps over the lea,
  A7    D      A    D  D7 G  A7       D
The sweet-scented birk shades my Mary and me.
```

```
        D    A7    D      G       D
Thy crystal stream Afton, how lovely it glides,
  A7   D     A7  D              E7  A
And winds by the cot where my Mary resides.
  A7    D A7 D        G       D
How wanton thy waters her snowy feet lave,
  A7   D        A     D  D7 G  A7           D
As gath'ring sweet flow'rets, she stems thy clear wave.
      A                  E7            A
Flow gently, sweet Afton, among thy green braes,
                          E7       A
Flow gently, sweet river, the theme of my lays.
  A7    D   F#7 Bm    D     G      D
My Mary's  asleep  by the murmuring stream,
  A7   D     A    D D7 G  A7        D
Flow gently, sweet Afton, disturb not her dreams.
```

87

I'm O'er Young

By Robert Burns

Chorus C

I'm o'er young I'm o'er___ young I'm o'er young to mar-ry yet! I'm

C   F   C   G   *Fine*

o'er young, 'twad be a sin To tak me frae my mam-mie yet.

C   Am   F   C   G7

I am my mam - mie's ae___ bairn, Wi' un - co folk I wear-y, sir And

C   Am   F   C   G7

ly - ing in a man's___ bed I'm fley'd it make me ee - rie, sir.

     C   Am
Hallowmass is come and gane,
         F   C   G7
The nights are lang in winter, Sir,
     C   Am
And you an' I in ae bed,
         F   C   G7
In trowth, I dare na venture, Sir!   *Chorus*

     C   Am
Fu' loud and shrill the frosty wind
         F   C   G7
Blaws thro' the leafless timmer, Sir,
     C   Am
But if ye come this gate again,
         F   C   G7
I'll aulder be gin simmer, Sir.   *Chorus*

ae bairn—only child   **unco**—strange

For the Sake o' Somebody

By Robert Burns

My heart is sair, I dare not tell,__ My heart is sair for Some - bod - y, I could wake a win - ter night __ For the sake o' Some - bod - y. O - hon! for Some - bod-y! O - hey! for Some - bod-y! I could range tle world a - round For the sake o' Some - bod - y.

E   B7
Ye powers that smile on virtuous love,
     E   A   E
O, sweetly smile on Somebody!
                 B7
Frae ilka danger keep him free,
     C#m   E
And send me safe my Somebody!
A   E
O-hon! for Somebody!
B7 E   B7
O-hey! for Somebody!
E   F#m   C#m G#m
I wad do — what wad I not?
   A   C#m   E
For the sake o' Somebody!

My Dowrie's the Jewel

By Robert Burns

O, much thinks my love o' my beau-ty, And much thinks my love o' my kin; But lit-tle thinks my love I ken-braw-lie My dow-rie's the jew-el has charms for him. It's a' for the ap-ple he'll nour-ish the tree, It's a' for the hon-ey he'll cher-ish the bee! My lad-die's sae much in love wi' the sil-ler, He can-na hae love to spare for me!

Dm
Your proffer o' love's an **airle-penny**,
F   C
My dowrie's the bargain ye wad buy;
Dm
But an ye be crafty, I am cunnin,
Am   Dm
Sae ye with ainther your fortune may try.

F   B
Ye're like to the timmer o' yon rotten wood,

F   Dm   C
Ye're like to the bark o' yon rotten tree:
Dm
Ye'll slip frae me like a knotless thread,
Am   Dm
An'ye'll crack ye're credit wi' mair nor me!

airle-penny—a worthless token
I ken brawlie—I know well

siller—silver
wi' mair nor me—with someone other than me

92

We're a' Noddin'

By Robert Burns

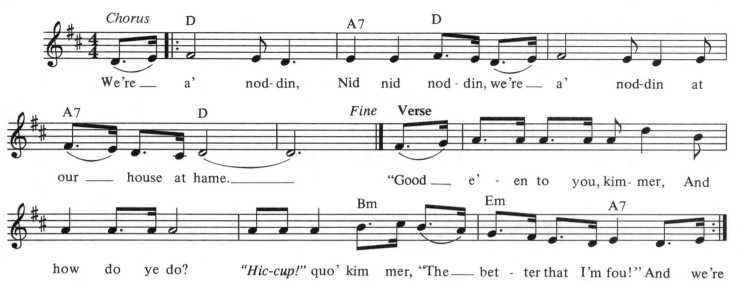

Chorus

We're ___ a' nod-din, Nid nid nod-din, we're ___ a' nod-din at our ___ house at hame.___ "Good ___ e' - en to you, kim-mer, And how do ye do? *"Hic-cup!"* quo' kim mer, "The ___ bet - ter that I'm fou!" And we're

D
Kate sits i' the neuk,

Suppin hen-broo.
    Bm
Deil tak Kate
  Em   **A7**
An she be na noddin too ! *Chorus*

D
"How's a' wi' you, kimmer?

And how do you fare?"
    Bm
"A pint o' the best o't,
  Em   **A7**
And twa pints mair!" *Chorus*

D
"How's a' wi' you, kimmer?

And how do ye thrive?
    Bm
How monie bairns hae ye?"
  Em   **A7**
Quo' kimmer, "I hae five." *Chorus*

D
"Are they a' Johnie's?"

"Eh! atweel na:
    Bm
Twa o' them were gotten
  Em   **A7**
When Johnie was awa!" *Chorus*

D
Cats like milk,

And dogs like broo;
    Bm
Lads like lasses weel,
  Em   **A7**
And lasses lads too. *Chorus*

atweel—in truth   **bairns**—children   **hen-broo**—chicken soup   **kimmer**—a married woman, a gossip

Corn Rigs

By Robert Burns

```
D7   G                D7
The sky was blue, the wind was still,
      G                Em D7
The moon was shining clearly;
G              D
I set her down, wi' right good will,
      C      D7    G D7 G
Amang the rigs o' barley:
           Em        D7
I ken't her heart was a' my ain;
    G         Em A7 D7
I lov'd her most sincerely;
    G     Em      Am     D
I kiss'd her owre and owre again,
     C    D7    G D7 G
Amang the rigs o' barley.   Chorus
```

```
D7 G                   D7
I lock'd her in my fond embrace;
       G              Em D7
Her heart was beating rarely:
     G              D
My blessings on that happy place,
      C      D7    G D7 G
Amang the rigs o' barley!
              Em        D7
But by the moon and stars so bright,
        G              Em A7 D7
That shone that hour so clearly!
      G     Em     Am      D
She ay shall bless that happy night
      C      D7    G D7 G
Amang the rigs o' barley.   Chorus
```

```
D7 G                       D7
I hae been blythe wi' comrades dear;
       G            Em D7
I hae been merry drinking;
       G             D
I hae been joyfu' gath'rin gear;
       C       D7    G D7 G
I hae been happy thinking:
              Em        D7
But a' the pleasures e'er I saw,
        G              Em A7 D7
Tho' three times doubl'd fairly,
        G     Em      Am        D
That happy night was worth them a',
      C      D7   G D7 G
Amang the rigs o' barley.   Chorus
```

Sodger Laddie

By Robert Burns

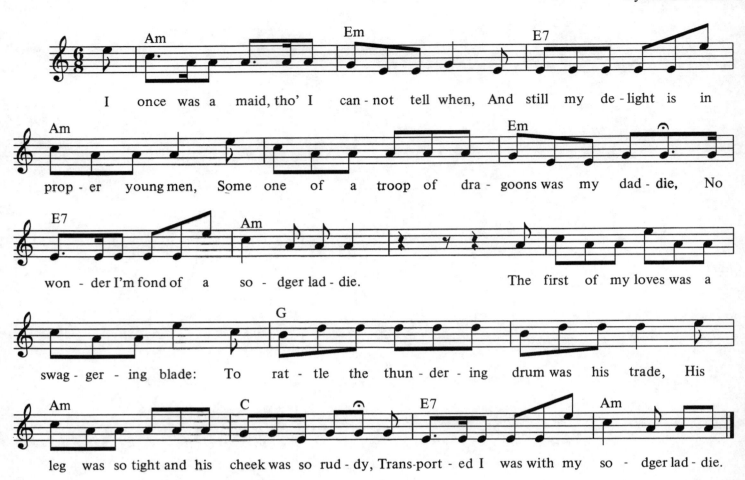

I once was a maid, tho' I can-not tell when, And still my de-light is in
prop-er young men, Some one of a troop of dra-goons was my dad-die, No
won-der I'm fond of a so-dger lad-die. The first of my loves was a
swag-ger-ing blade: To rat-tle the thun-der-ing drum was his trade, His
leg was so tight and his cheek was so rud-dy, Trans-port-ed I was with my so-dger lad-die.

Am   Em
But the godly old chaplain left him in the lurch;
E7   Am
The sword I forsook for the sake of the church;
          Em
He risked the soul, and I ventur'd the body:
E7   Am
'Twas then I prov'd false to my sodger laddie.

Full soon I grew sick of my sanctified sot;
  G
The regiment at large for a husband I got;
         Am   C
From the gilded spontoon to the fife I was ready;
E7   Am
I asked no more but a sodger laddie.

       Am   Em
But the peace it reduc'd me to beg in despair,
E7   Am
'Til I met my old boy in a Cunningham Fair,
          Em
His rags regimental they flutter'd so gaudy:
E7   Am
My heart it rejoic'd at a sodger laddie.

And now I have liv'd — I know not how long!
  G
But still I can join in a cup and a song;
         Am   C
And whilst with both hands I can hold the glass steady,
E7   Am
Here's to thee, my hero, my sodger laddie!

spontoon—a kind of halberd (a battle axe on a long pike)

Wanderin' Willie

By Robert Burns

Here a - wa,___ there a - wa, wan - der - ing Wil - lie,___

Here a - wa,___ there a - wa, haud a - wa hame!

Come to my bos - om, my ae ——— on - ly dear - ie,___ And

tell me thou bring'st me my Wil - lie the same.

C Am E7 Am
Loud tho' the Winter blew cauld at our parting,
C Am Dm Am
'Twas na the blast brought the tear in my e'e:
  E7 F C
Welcome now Simmer, and welcome my Willie,
 Am E7 Am E7 Am
The Simmer to Nature, my Willie to me!

C Am E7 Am
Rest, ye wild storms in the cave o' your slumbers —
C Am Dm Am
How your wild howling a lover alarms!
  E7 F C
Wauken, ye breezes, row gently, ye billows,
  Am E7 Am E7 Am
And waft my dear laddie ance mair to my arms.

  C Am E7 Am
But O, if he's faithless, and minds na his Nannie,
  C Am Dm Am
Flow still between us, thou wide-roaring main!
  E7 F C
May I never see it, may I never trow it,
  Am E7 Am E7 Am
But, dying, believe that my Willie's my ain!

The Highland Widow's Lament

"I ken, when we had a King, and a chancellor and Parliament—men o' our ain, we could peeble them wi' stanes when they werena gude bairns. But naebody's nails can reach the length o' Lunnon." (Sir Walter Scott, *The Heart of Midlothian*)

By Robert Burns

O, I am come to the low coun-trie, O-chon, o-chon, o-chrie! ____ With-out a pen-ny in ____ my purse to buy a meal __ to me. ____

Em Bm C Bm
It was na sae in the Highland hills,
G Bm C G
Ochon, ochon, ochrie!
Em C G Em
Nae woman in the country wide,
G Em C G
Sae happy was as me.

Em Bm C Bm
For then I had a score o' kye,
G Bm C G
Ochon, ochon, ochrie!
Em C G Em
Feeding on yon hill sae high
G Em C G
And giving milk to me.

Em Bm C Bm
And there I had three score o' yowes,
G Bm C G
Ochon, ochon, ochrie!
Em C G Em
Skipping on yon bonie knowes
G Em C G
And casting woo' to me.

Em Bm C G
I was the happiest of a' the clan,
G Bm C G
Sair, sair may I repine!
Em C G Em
For Donald was the brawest man,
Gm Em C G
And Donald he was mine.

Em Bm C Bm
Till Charlie Stewart cam at last,
G Bm C G
Sae far to set us free:
Em C G Em
My Donald's arm was wanted then,
G Em C G
For Scotland and for me.

Em Bm C Bm
Their waefu' fate what need I tell?
G Bm C G
Right to the wrang did yield:
Em C G Em
My Donald and his country fell
G Em C G
Upon Culloden field.

Em Bm C Bm
Ochon! Ochon! O Donald, O!
G Bm C G
Ochon, ochon, ochrie!
Em C G Em
Nae woman in the warld wide
G Em C G
Sae wretched now as me!

brawest—handsomest   **knowes**—knolls   **kye**—cows   **yowes**—sheep, ewes

John Anderson, My Jo

By Robert Burns

John An - der - son my jo, John when __ we were first ac - quent, Your

locks were like the ra - ven, your bo - nie brow was brent; But

now your brow is beld, John, your locks are like the snaw, But __

bless - ings on your fros - ty pow, John An - der - son my jo!

    Em Am   Em
John Anderson my jo, John,
      A7   D
I wonder what ye mean,
    Em Am   Em
To lie so long in the morning,
  G D7 G
And sit so late at e'en.
       Em   Bm
You're bleary at your eye, John,
   Am   B7
And why do ye so,
     Em   D   Em
Come sooner to your bed at e'en?
       D   Em
John Anderson my jo!

    Em Am   Em
John Anderson my jo, John,
      A7   D
You're welcome when ye please.
    Em Am   Em
It's either in the warm bed,
  G D7   G
Or else above the claes.
    Em   Bm
Do ye your part above, John,
   Am   B7
And trust to me below—
     Em   D Em
I've twa gae ups to your gae doon,
       D   Em
John Anderson my jo!

     Em Am   Em
John Anderson my jo, John,
       A7   D
We clamb the hill thegither,
     Em Am   Em
And monie a cantie day, John,
   G D7 G
We've had wi' ane anither.
      Em   Bm
Now we maun totter down, John,
    Am   B7
And hand in hand we'll go,
      Em   D Em
And sleep thegither at the foot,
        D   Em
John Anderson, my jo!

claes—(bed)clothes   **jo**—sweetheart   **pow**—the head

Kellyburn Braes

By Robert Burns

There lived___ a carl___ in Kel - ly-burn-braes, Hey and the rue___ grows

bo - nie wi' thyme; And he had a wife was the plague o' his days, And the

thyme it is with-er'd and rue is in prime, And rue is in prime.

Follow the pattern of the first verse

C
Ae day as the carl gaed up the lang-glen . . .
Am   Em   F   C
He met wi' the devil, says, how do ye fen?. .

C
I've got a bad wife, Sir, that's a' my complaint · · ·
Am   Em   F   C
For, saving your presence, to her ye're a saint . . .

C
It's neither your stot nor your staig I shall crave · · ·
Am   Em   F   C
But gie me your wife, man, for her I must have · · ·

C
O, welcome most kindly! the blythe carl said. . .
Am   Em   F   C
But if ye can match her-ye're waur than ye're ca'd · · ·

C
The devil has got the auld wife on his back. . .
Am   Em   F   C
And like a poor pedlar he's carried his pack. . .

C
He's carried her hame to his ain hallan-door. . .
Am   Em   F   C
Syne bade her gae in wi' a terrible roor. . .

C
Then straight he makes fifty, the pick o' his band. . .
Am   Em   F   C
Turn out on her guard in the clap of a hand . . .

C
The carlin gaed thro' them like onie wud bear. . .
Am   Em   F   C
Whae'er she gat hands on, cam near her nae mair. . .

C
A reekit, wee devil looks over the wa' · · ·
Am   Em   F   C
O help, Master, help! or she'll ruin us a . . .

C
The devil he swore by the edge o' his knife. . .
Am   Em   F   C
He pitied the man that was ty'd to a wife. . .

C
The devil he swore by the kirk and the bell. . .
Am   Em   F   C
He was not in wedlock, thank Heaven, but in hell. . .

C
Then Satan has travell'd again wi' his pack. . .
Am   Em   F   C
And to her auld husband he's carried her back. . .

C
I hae been a devil the most o' my life. . .
Am   Em   F   C
But neer was in hell till I met wi' your wife. ..

carl—an old fellow   hallan—partition between cottage door and fireplace   stot—young bullock
carlin—old wife   reekit—smoky   waur—worse
fen—do   staig—young horse   wud—mad

Braw Lads o' Galla Water

By Robert Burns

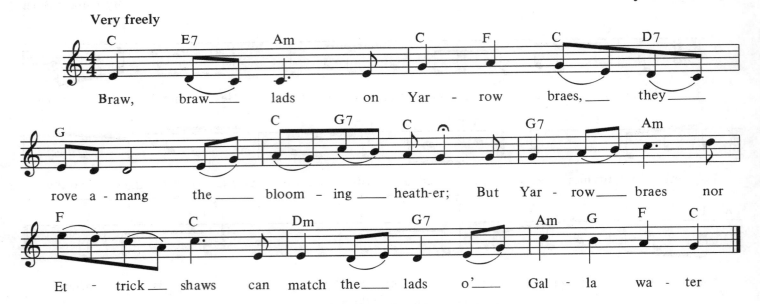

Very freely

Braw, braw lads on Yar - row braes, they rove a - mang the bloom - ing heath-er; But Yar - row braes nor Et - trick shaws can match the lads o' Gal - la wa - ter

C E7   Am   C F   C
But there is ane, a secret ane,
D7 G   C G7 C
Aboon them a' I loe him better;
    G7 Am   F   C
And I'll be his, and he'll be mine,
    Dm G7 Am G F C
The bonie lad o' Galla Water.

C E7   Am   C F C
Altho' his daddie was nae laird,
 D7 G   C G7 C
And tho' I hae nae meikle tocher,
    G7 Am   F   C
Yet, rich in kindest truest love,
      Dm   G7   Am G F C
We'll tent our flocks by Galla Water.

C E7   Am   C F C
It ne'er was wealth, it ne'er was wealth,
   D7 G   C   G7   C
That coft contentment, peace, and pleasure;
     G7   Am   F   C
The bands and bliss o' mutual love,
     Dm   G7   Am G F C
O, that's the chiefest warld's treasure!

Braw—Handsome   **coft**—bought   **nae meikle tocher**—not much (of a) dowry

Scots Wha Hae

Robert Burns: "Independently of my enthusiams as a Scotsman, I have rarely met with anything in history which interests my feelings as a man equal with the story of Bannockburn [the battle of Bannockburn, June 24, 1314, in which Robert Bruce defeated the English under Edward II]. On the one hand, a cruel but able usurper, leading on the finest army in Europe, to extinguish the last spark of freedom among a greatly-daring and greatly-injured people; on the other hand, the desperate relics of a gallant nation, devoting themselves to rescue their bleeding country or perish with her. Liberty! thou art a prize truly and indeed invaluable, for never canst thou be too dearly bought."

William Wallace (c. 1270–1305) led his Scottish army in the victorious battle at Stirling Bridge on the Forth on September 11, 1297. His infantry massacred the attacking British mounted knights. Though he strove mightily to drive the British from Scotland he was eventually captured and executed in London.

Robert Bruce (1274–1329) fought alongside Wallace against Edward II, and after Wallace's death continued to battle for an independent Scotland. He was crowned Robert I, King of Scotland, on March 27, 1306. His ancestor, Robert de Brus, had come over from Normandy with William the Conqueror in 1066. Robert's daughter, Marjory, married Walter, High Steward of Scotland. Their son Robert adopted his father's title as his name and, as Robert II, founded the Stuart dynasty.

By Robert Burns

Scots wha hae wi' Wallace bled, Scots wham Bruce has of-ten led,___
Wel - come to your gor - y bed, Or to vic - to - ry!
Now's the day and now's the hour, See the front of bat - tle lour,
See ap - proach proud Ed-ward's pow'r, Chains and slav - er - y.

G
Wha will be a traitor knave?
C
Wha can fill a coward's grave?
G   B7   Em
Wha sae base as be a slave?
C   G
Let him turn and flee!

Wha, for Scotland's king and law,
D
Freedom's sword will strongly draw,
G   B7   Em
Freeman stand or Freeman fa',
C   G
Let them follow me!

G
By oppression's woes and pains,
C
By your sons in servile chains,
G   B7   Em
We will drain our dearest veins,
C   G
But they shall be free.

Lay the proud usurpers low!
D
Tyrants fall in ev'ry foe!
G   B7   Em
Liberty's in ev'ry blow!
C   G
Let us do or die!

The Wee Magic Stane

On Christmas day in 1950 some young Scottish people successfully made off with the famed Coronation Stone from Westminster Abbey. It was an act of Scottish nationalism not without humorous overtones, set down here to the tune of "Villikins and His Dinah," better known in America as "Sweet Betsy from Pike."

The dean of West-min-ster wis a pow-er-ful man, He held a' the reins o' the state in his hand, His pow-er did come from a stane wi' a ring, For with oot it, it seems we'd be want-in' a king.

Chorus

Sing-in' oo-ra-li, oo-ra-li, oo-ra-li ay.

D   A7   D
But wi' a' this fine business, it flustert him nane,
             E7   A
Till some rogues ran away wi' his wee magic stane,
Bm   F#m   G   D
So he sent for the polis' and gave this decree,
              A7   D
"Go and bring back the stane and return it to me." *Chorus*

D   A7   D
The polis' went beetlin' up tae the north,
          E7   A
They huntit the Clyde and they huntit the Forth,
Bm   F#m   G   D
But the wild folks up yonder they kiddit them a',
          A7   D
For they didna believe it was magic at a'. *Chorus*

D   A7   D
Now the Provost of Glesca', Sir Victor by name,
    E7   A
Was awfi' put oot when he heard o' the stane,
Bm   F#m   G   D
So he sent for the statues that stand i' the Square,
          A7   D
That the high church's masons might mak' a few mair. *Chorus*

D   A7   D
When the Dean o' Westminster with this wis acquaint,
          E7   A
He sent for Sir Victor and made him a Saint.
          Bm   F#m   G   D
"Now it's nae use ye sendin' yer statues doon here,"
             A7   D
Said the Dean, "But ye've gaid me a reet guid idea." *Chorus*

D   A7   D
So he sent for a stane o' the verra same stuff,
         E7   A
And he had it drest up till it looked like enough,
         Bm   F#m   G   D
Then he sent for the Press and announced that the stane
          A7   D
Had been found and returned to Westminster again. *Chorus*

D   A7   D
When the reevers found oot what Westminster had done,
         E7   A
They started to turn oot the stanes by the ton,
         Bm   F#m   G   D
And for each yin they finished they enter the claim,
          A7   D
That this wis the true and original stane. *Chorus*

      D   A7   D
But the cream o' the jest still remains to be telt,
                    E7   A
For the man who wis turnin' 'em oot on the belt,
    Bm   F♯m   G   D
At the peak o' production wis sae sairly prest,
      D   A7   D
That the real yin got bunged in along wi' the rest. *Chorus*

         D   A7   D
So if ever ye come on a stane wi' a ring,
              E7   A
Just sit yersel' doon and appoint yersel' king,
         Bm   F♯m   G   D
For ther's none will be able tae challenge yer claim,
                A7   D
That ye crownt yersel' king on the Destiny Stane. *Chorus*

The Coronation Coronach

The Scottish Republican movement of the 1950s turned to biting satire in its songs. "Everything was thrown into the pot: The missionaries first to give it the bite, army ballads from World War II, football songs, Orange songs, Fenian songs, Child ballads, street songs, children's songs, bothy ballads, blues, skiffle, Australian bush ballads, calypsos, MacColl and Lomax, Ives and Leadbelly, songs about the Stone of Destiny, Dominic Behan, S.R.A. songs, I.R.A. songs, Guthrie and Houston, pantomime and vaudeville, Billy Graham, Scottish Land League songs, Gaelic songs and mouth music, Wobbly songs, spirituals, mountaineering and hiking ballads, Elliot and Seeger...the Royal Family...." (From the liner notes to *Ding, Dong Dollar,* a 1962 Folkways recording.)

Noo, Scotland has nae got a king, And she Has nae got a queen. For ye canna hae the second Liz when the first one's never been. Nae Liz the Twa, nae Lilibet the Wan, nae Liz will ever dae. For we'll mak oor land Republican in a Scottish breakaway.

D7 G
Noo her man's cried the Duke of Edinburgh—
Am   D7
He's wan o yon kilty Greeks.

Here, but dinnae blaw my kilts awa,
G   C   D7 G
For it's Lizzie wears the breeks. *Chorus*

D7 G
He's handsome, man, looks like Don Juan;
Am   D7
He's beloved by the weaker sex.

But it disnae really matter a damn,
G   C D7 G
For it's Lizzie signs the cheques. *Chorus*

D7   G
Noo her sister Meg's got a bonny pair o legs,
Am   D7
But she didna want a German or a Greek.

Puir auld Peter was her choice, but he didnae suit the boys,
G   C D7 G
So they selt him up the creek. *Chorus*

D7   G
Here, but Meg was fly, and she beat them by and by
Am   D7
Wi Tony Hyphenated-Armstrong.

But behind the pomp an play, the question of the day
G   C D7 G
Was, who the hell did Suzy Wong? *Chorus*

D7 G
Sae here's tae the Lion, tae the bonny Rampant Lion,
Am   D7
And a lang streetch tae its paw.

Gie a Hampden roar, and it's oot the door,
G   C D7 G
And ta-ta tae Chairlie's maw. *Chorus*

Coronach—lamentation or dirge for the dead which accompanied funerals in the Highlands

Ding Dong Dollar

The Scotsman (Edinburgh, Monday, May 22, 1961): WET WELCOME ON THE LOCH . . . *Proteus* sailors turn hoses on anti-Polaris canoeists. . . . With a barrage of fire hoses, the United States Navy yesterday repulsed the seaborne invasion of anti-Polaris [nuclear submarine] demonstrators who tried to board the submarine depot ship, *Proteus,* in the Holy Loch. . . . Members of Scottish Council for Nuclear Disarmament lit a bonfire on the beach . . . and settled down for an all-night vigil.

O ye can-ny spend a dol-lar when ye're deid, O ye can-ny spends a dol-lar when ye're deid; Sing-in Ding-Dong-Dol-lar; Ev-'ry bod-y hol-ler: Ye can-ny spend a dol-lar when Ye're deid.

Final Chorus

    G
O the Yanks have juist drapt anchor in Dunoon,
                                      D7
An' they've had their civic welcome frae the toon,
             G
As they came up the measured mile,
        C
Bonnie Mary o' Argyll
      G   D7   G
Wis wearin spangled drawers ablow her goun.   *Chorus*

         G
An the publicans will aa be daein swell,
                             D7
For it's juist the thing that's sure tae ring the bell,
        G
O the dollars they will jingle,
        C
They'll be no lassie single,
      G   D7   G
Even though they maybe blaw us aa tae hell.   *Chorus*

         G
But the Glesca Moderator disnae mind;
                                      D7
In fact, he thinks the Yanks are awfy kind,
         G
For if it's heaven that ye're goin,
        C
It's a quicker way than rowin,
      G   D7   G
An there's sure tae be naebody left behind.   *Chorus*

There is a particularly touching children's song to the same tune, which by the way is "She'll Be Coming 'Round the Mountain":

         G
O, ye canny push your granny off a bus,
                                  D7
O, ye canny push your granny off a bus,
         G
O, ye canny push your granny,
        C
For she is your mammy's mammy —
      G   D7   G
O, ye canny push your granny off a bus.